"Patron on Ice: 1

Text TBRS to 95577 to subscribe to the mailing list for updates!

Written by David Weaver

RHONDO

"I don't wanna do that shit no more Reecy Pooh. I'm done man fuck that shit." I said as I pushed my wheelchair back from the table and closed my eyes, exhausted. I'd been shot 5 times, and was trying my best to recover being that one of the places I got hit was in my head. They had me doing homework and shit like I was in kindergarten all over again.

"Baby listen. I know you're frustrated, but we have to get through this ordeal together. As a team. You always said you wanted a ride or die chick, and here I am... riding with you no matter what. All I ask is that you match my effort."

My woman's voice was calm, soft, and soothing, very different from the ghetto tone she normally had with me, so I knew she was trying to have patience because of my situation. It seemed like no matter how many times I'd given up trying to learn how to do simple shit again, she was always pushing me to go harder. She never let me throw the towel in.

"Reecy Pooh, I'm tired." I pleaded. "And I'm in pain. I don't wanna' sit here doing no damn homework right now."

She kneeled down and placed her hands on my knees, staring me in the eyes. "Rhondo I know you're tired, in pain, all that shit. But baby I'm working just as hard as you, don't forget about that... Don't forget all of the work I'm putting in to make sure you're straight. You see me grinding for us... Don't you?"

She was right. I was being an ass when I didn't have any right to be complaining. Them fuck niggas' tried to take me out and here I was still breathing, still pushing, still able to be around my beautiful girlfriend, so what was I so angry about?

I nodded my head and smiled at Reecy Pooh. "You're right Ma. Let me try this again."

My Reecy pushed me back up to the table and watched me as I reached my hand out in an attempt to grab the pencil that was laying on the desk. Every time I tried to grab the pencil, it seemed to fumble and roll away. I started getting more and more frustrated because I'd just grabbed the pencil earlier, and was even able to write with it, and here I was now unable to close my hand around it to repeat the task.

Reecy picked the pencil up and tried to place it in my hand and I nudged it away with my arm. "I can do it myself Reecy!" I screamed, instantly feeling bad.

Reecy bent down and picked the pencil up calmly. She placed it back on the table and walked away. I could tell that I'd hurt her feelings, but I hated the fact that I couldn't do something as simple as picking up a got damn pencil. That shit was fuckin with me something serious. I knew I'd been rude to her, but I really needed to be able to just pick up the pencil on my own so that I could have a peace of mind.

I tried again to pick it up, and was having no luck. Reecy came back out and sat on the sofa with her laptop, her notebooks, and her glasses. She had been going to school to be a nurse, while I was out running the streets trying to be the fuckin King of Atlanta.

I tried again to pick up the pencil and finally something clicked in my brain, allowing me to pick the pencil up. A small surge of happiness went through me, and I started feeling better about my progress again. I pressed the pencil down against the paper and traced the dotted design of my name, so I could get the hang of writing it again. Then I went back to the problem I was having trouble with. I read it aloud, slowly...

"Ooooone. T-two. F-f-f-fourrrr. Si-Si-Sixxxx. T-t-t-ttttt..." I took a deep breath in frustration. I know what the word was but my brain didn't wanna spit it out. "T-t-t-teeeeen."

I exhaled and looked over at Reecy Pooh to see if she was going to come help me, but she was paying me no attention. I felt bad because she was only trying to help me and I was giving her such a difficult time. I looked back at the paper. It looked so foreign to me that I forgot what was going on. I closed my eyes and dropped the pencil against the table. A tear fell from my eye and rolled down my cheek. I sighed and thought back to the day they tried to kill me. I tried to remember the shooter's voice again, but I was having difficulty in doing so.

Reecy Pooh kissed my tear away gently. I opened my eyes and saw that she was crying too. I wished that I could have held her but I was in so much pain... I could barely hold a pencil.

"Rhondo we gon get through this shit bae. I know it's hard, shit I already know how you are. But you gotta stop fighting me and let me help you the best way I know how. I'm here for you, I didn't abandon you like your friends."

Her words cut me deep, although I know she didn't mean it to be taken that way. Suddenly I could remember the shooter's voice again. The shooter had been somebody I'd once considered a friend. A nigga named Mac who I'd let borrow money when he was down on his dick one time. A nigga who I let stay at one of my apartments when he was on the run one time... A nigga who I sent money to while he did a 3-year prison bid... That nigga came home and tried to kill me. I was more determined to complete my homework so I could get back to these streets. I reached for the pencil again, and picked it up effortlessly this time, surprised.

I stared at the sheet of paper, and looked at Reecy Pooh for help.

"Rhondo it says fill in the blanks of the missing numbers."

I stared at it blankly, unable to process what they were talking about. My mind was fuzzy again, and I forgot the shooter's voice again. I forgot what I was doing, and the pencil fell out of my hand and rolled off of the table. A pain seemed to start in my neck and quickly spread to my head. I frowned in excruciating pain, showing all of my teeth in my expression.

"Baby let me get your pain pills and get you in the bed. Let's pick this back up when you wake up. It has been 8 hours since you last took pills. You're doing better because one time you couldn't go 4 hours without taking them. Your body is healing." Reecy said, encouraging me.

"I love you Rhondo." She said as she went to get my meds.

I heard her but was in too much pain to reply. My mind was fuzzy, and then it was clear again. I saw my shooter again, heard his voice, heard the gunshots, and my mind went blank again. I saw the hospital, heard the nurse, heard the doctor, and remembered the blackness again. I relaxed in the wheelchair, unable to control anything, and barely able to breathe. I saw light with my eyes closed, and then darkness again.

REECY POOH

I loved my nigga, but got damn Rhondo gave me such a hard time. I stood by that nigga through so much crazy ass shit, and not once had he ever made an effort to marry me and give me his raggedy ass last name. I done stood by this nigga from jail time to me literally beating his side bitch's ass, from him getting us all robbed at gunpoint to this nigga being shot up and on his death bed. After all of that shit he put me through, all he'd ever given me was a got damn STD. I knew I deserved better than that.

The crazy thing was... I was about to break the news to his ass that I was leaving him on the day that he got shot. I'd talked about it with my girlfriends, and practiced saying the shit in the mirror the whole week. Then with my crazy ass luck, his ass gets shot up in traffic and left for dead. I couldn't leave him then. My heart wouldn't let me do him like that, especially when I knew he had nobody else he could trust in his corner.

On top of that, a bullet had hit him in the head, making his memory go in and out. The doctor said that with repetition of the basics, that he'd eventually be back to normal, but I would have to be extremely patient and work with him. Shit if you ask me, his ass always forgot the basics, with a bullet or without a bullet.

The basics according to me:
1) *Stop cheating on me nigga.*
2) *Stop tryna sell dope. It's not working for you.*
3) *Stop trusting all these niggas.*
4) *Stop fucking all these bitches raw!*

Man that nigga forgot the basics every damn day, shit.

I stood in the mirror and applied final touches to my makeup, to make sure it was perfect, and I grabbed my Coulisse Palazzo Empire Versace bag off of the bed. That bag cost me $3,200 and it damn sholl' didn't come from my nigga selling dope. It came from me putting my own work in with my own hustle. I walked out of the bedroom, grabbed the keys to my 2004 BMW, and kissed Rhondo on the cheek.

I'd given him a Percocet, so he was definitely going to be out on the couch for a while, allowing me to go handle my business real quick. I hurried out the house, locked the door, and checked the time. I needed to be sure to be home by a certain time in case he woke up soon. I backed my car up and took off.

PATRON

I parked my truck besides the mailbox by the first house on the street. My co-worker jumped out while I was looking through my phone for the resident's phone number. Before I could find it, my co-worker had already started the lawn mower and was getting started with the task at hand. I called the number, and when the older lady answered it, I rolled my window up and stuck one finger in my other ear while I took the phone call.

"Hello?" She asked in a low whiny voice. She almost sounded as if I was irritating her.

"Yes ma'am. This is Patrick. I came to cut your grass."

"Hello?" She asked again.

"Ma'am this is Patrick," I yelled louder so she could hear me, "I came to—"

"Ohhh Patrick. Ok sweetheart. I have some fresh lemonade in here if you guys get thirsty. Watch out for snakes out there."

"Yes ma'am! Thank you!"

I got out and grabbed the weed-eater, and proceeded to help my guys finish the job.

While trimming down the hedges, I thought about the girl I had a crush on, and wondered how many lawns I'd have to service in order to be the type of guy she would pay attention to. She was getting money on her own, so it was so hard for dudes like me... Just regular working dudes with lawn services, and it was a shame because I really liked her... I thought she was one of the most beautiful women I'd ever laid eyes on.

Her name was Ice, and she was a booster, but she was one of the best the city of Atlanta had ever seen. She seemed to have everything for sale, and anybody in the city knew that if they wanted the best prices on stuff, that she was the person to get it from. I thought about her smile and how nice she smelled, and I knew that as soon as I got through with my day, I was going to go buy some new gear from her just to try to impress her.

I'd spent so much money with her that it was pitiful. I had a room full of clothes and shoes I'd bought from her that I'd never even worn before. It was beginning to feel like I was working just to be able to pay for the stuff. A part of me knew that I shouldn't be spending all of my money on a woman who has no interest in me, but another part of me refused to not support her. I felt like she was my woman, whether she felt the same way or not, and I figured as long as I was supporting her, then I could make sure that she didn't need anybody for nothing and would always have a place to lay her head.

"Patron!" My co-worker yelled. "You're going to get even darker than you already are standing in that one spot like that."

I was in a trance staring at a bush while thinking about Ice. "My bad Jose. I had some shit on my mind." I said, apologizing to my Mexican friend.

He looked at me and smirked. "It's ok amigo. We all worry about stuff we have no control over."

As soon as he said it, I thought about the possibility of him getting deported and felt bad. I was worrying about my problems without even thinking of my Mexican friend who'd helped me build my lawn service from scratch. "No worries Jose. You're going to be fine. Let's get this money. We're going to build an empire one day, and you won't ever have to worry again."

ICE

"Yes ma'am. I like this watch and the bracelet. How much was it again?" I asked while handing it back to her.

She grabbed the watch, and pulled the tag from the inside of it. "This is a Rolex with 1 full karat of diamonds. Keep in mind we also have them without diamonds in them. However, this watch is $23,000, but I can give it to you for $22,500. I can't give much of a discount on this item." She said while switching the watch to her other hand and then reading the tag on the bracelet.

"This bracelet is 2 full karats of *VS* quality diamonds, and it retails for $10,000. However, since you're such a good customer, I can give it to you for $7,500." She said while staring at me over her glasses.

I glanced at Reecy Pooh to see what her reaction was going to be. Me and her had been stealing shit all damn day, and I didn't know if we had reached our limit yet, but when I saw her reaching into her wallet, I figured we still had room for more despite us having several bags of items valued at at least $200,000.

"I think it's a great deal Ice." Reecy Pooh said as she handed me a credit card to use.

I grabbed a card and smiled at the salesperson. "I'll take both of them please."

The salesperson was too eager to make her commission off of the items, and I was just as eager to make the transaction happen so I could get the fuck up out of there. As always, I was nervous as hell, and I just needed things to go smoothly. Reecy Pooh picked up the remainder of the bags while I walked to the counter to handle my business.

"Ice, I'll take these to the car, and wait on you ok?" Reecy said.

I simply nodded my head as she carried the items out of the store. I sat on the stool in front of the cashier and smiled as she processed the transaction on her computer. "Could I see your ID ma'am?" She asked.

"Yes of course." I said as I grabbed the ID out of my purse and handed it to her.

"Thanks Victoria." She said.

It was a fake ID for sure, but it matched the name on the stolen credit card. My real name was Iclyis, and my friends called me Ice but of course I would never offer that information. I sat patiently as she prepared to run the card. I glanced at the mirror in the top corner of the store at the reflection of the armed guard standing by the door. It took a lot of courage and guts to do what me and Reecy did on a monthly basis.

She ran the credit card and after a moment, she started placing the items in a gift box, and then placed them in the gift bag. She reached under the counter to grab a jewelry cleaning cloth, and then froze in place. She placed the cleaning cloth down, picked the card up and swiped it again. My heart was beating out of my chest, and I could barely remember breathing during those moments.

"Is there anything wrong?" I asked the salesperson, my palms sweating and my arms shaking.

"Well... I've been having trouble with the machine all day, but it's saying here that the card is declined, and to call fraud protection."

I was so glad that Reecy Pooh grabbed those bags because I needed to be lightweight in case that situation called for me to have a very drastic response to the entire scenario. I didn't care about that guard at the door, I wasn't going to be taken to jail in a damn jewelry store. I was about to cook up a lie, when she followed up.

"Have you done a lot of shopping today?" She asked while staring at me.

"Yes, I have." I replied calmly.

"Well maybe that's it. They probably put a block on your card until you verified some of your transactions. This is a large purchase, so maybe they suspected fraud. I'll hold the items while you call them." The saleslady said.

"O.K. Thank you." I said.

Her phone rang on the other side of the room, and I knew what was happening, even when she didn't.

"I'm about to go to the ATM outside of this store and see if my other card has the available balance." I said as I walked towards the door.

"OK, I'll be here." She said as she picked up the phone.

As soon as I got outside of the store, I took off running. Fuck the bullshit. I ran outside, and Reecy Pooh was parked right at the entrance waiting on me. The car door was open, so I jumped in, slammed the door and we were off.

"Shit bitch that was close!" I screamed as I sat back in the seat. Reecy drove the stolen car out of the Mall parking lot, onto Peachtree Street, drove down the street a couple of blocks, and valet parked the car at the W Hotel. We grabbed our bags, tipped the valet $200, and hopped into a waiting Uber. The Uber took us to Piedmont Road where we got out at Mama's Mexican restaurant, and took a Lyft to the Westin Hotel on Peachtree Street. We got in Reecy's car and both took deep breaths.

I looked through the bags while Reecy drove. I marveled at how good we were as a team. It wasn't even about the card being detected as fraud, it was about the merchandise we'd stolen. We'd swapped out the real watch and bracelet with the fake watch and bracelet right before the salesperson's eyes, and after the fact, I tried to purchase the fake watch with a stolen card that I knew wasn't going to work. We'd been maxed that card out weeks prior.

I held the $23,000 Rolex up and lusted at how beautiful the diamonds were. We'd hit Lennox for $100,000 in stolen watches that day, and nearly $200,000 in jewelry altogether during that trip. The other bags were of men's clothing, shoes, expensive purses, socks, make-up, and a few laptops. The purpose of the smaller items was for us to get some immediate cash while we worked on selling the larger ticket items. We had to make sure all of our bills were paid, and that we kept a constant cash flow while we waited on the ballers to cut that check with us.

I took a deep breath and smiled as Reecy drove her BMW down 85 South. We were headed to Cleveland Avenue to sell a few items so that we could take it in for the day. Reecy was my partner-in-crime and best friend, and we'd been riding it out for years. We had a beautiful chemistry and an amazing bond.

Jiip

"Nigga I fucked a bitch I met off the Instagram explorer page!" He screamed as he laughed out loud. His young homey, Albert, held his stomach while laughing at Jiip's joke.

"I'm so for real Al. Man I fucked that ho from the back and nutted in her hair. Shit she wanted some likes! I liked it! Lemme show you the bitch!" He screamed as he pulled out his cell phone.

"Man I'm telling you Al. It's one of them flat tummy tea ass hoes. Bitch is a photo shop pro because that bitch got so many stretch marks she could sell some! Man she got stretch marks on her feet nigga!"

Albert started laughing even harder. He looked up to Jiip, and wanted to be just like him, regardless of what it took. Just as Jiip was about to show Albert the girl's Instagram page, his phone rang. He quickly dismissed the call, and as his phone was refreshing, it rang again.

"Fuck!" He exclaimed. "Man lemme see what this bitch want. Hold on."

"Yea!" He screamed into the phone, his voice strong and hoarse, padded from all of the cigarettes he'd smoked over the years.

"Damn nigga! You trippin!" Reecy Pooh screamed into the phone.

"Bitch what you want?" He screamed while laughing like it was a joke.

"Quit calling me that shit nigga! I done told yo' punk ass one time." Reecy Pooh screamed back. She felt bad because she really cared for Jiip, but he just had no respect for women. He was, after all, the guy she was trying to leave Rhondo for.

"I'm sorry baby. You know you my bae." Jiip said, attempting to use a sweet voice. Hell, it was good enough for Reecy.

"Man... anyways... I got some Rolexes, shit what can you give me right now?" Reecy asked enthusiastically.

Jiip jumped up out of his seat and walked to the kitchen, so as to talk out of Albert's listening reach. "Shidddd how much they worth? They got diamonds or they plain janes?"

"Shit I got both nigga. At least $100,000 worth. Hell... how much you got for them?" Reecy asked.

Jiip thought for a minute. "Shit I got $20,000 on me right now." He said quietly.

"$20,000? Nigga you got me fucked up. You trippin! We need as least $40,000 nigga!" She screamed into the phone.

"Bitch bring your dumb ass over here and pick up this $20,000 like I told you and quit tryna front in front of that stupid ass hoe." He said and hung up the phone.

"The fuck... oughta be lucky I don't just take her shit." He said to himself as he sat in a chair and pulled his money out. He counted $20,000 out of the bankroll and put the rest of it back up. He had been a stick-up-kid since he was 13 years old, and the only reason he didn't rob Reecy Pooh was because he had way bigger plans for her.

He grabbed a bag out of the cabinet and placed the money in it. He grabbed his pistol and mask, and set off to go do a quick job to replace the money he was about to spend. He couldn't afford to take any losses. Money was hard to come by for him to even drop a dollar.

RHONDO

My cell phone seemed like it would never stop ringing. I glanced over and saw that it was in reach, but didn't feel confident that I was going to be able to answer it. Hell I had to give it a try though. Those bullets had really done a number on me, and I knew I needed to fight through it all in order to get revenge.

When I tried to move my arm, a sharp pain ran through it that was so strong that it made me shudder as if I was about to be shot again. I tried to move my arm again, in fear that the phone would stop ringing soon, and when I was finally able to reach out and touch the phone, it stopped ringing. I closed my eyes in disappointment, and when I was about to withdraw my hand from the phone, it started ringing again.

I fought through the pain, grabbed the phone and placed it to my ear.

"I'ma kill you, you bitch!" The voiced whispered in my ear. My eyes opened wide, and I tried to stare at the phone to see what the number was on it, but my eyes were too blurry. I figured it was because I was moving too fast and it was messing up my blood circulation. I closed my eyes again, and when I opened them, I saw Reecy Pooh walking in the house. I knew I had to be strong for my woman, so I put the phone back to my ear.

"Fuck you nigga! You ain't kill shit last time you hoe ass nigga!" I yelled into the phone.

Reecy Pooh walked up to me and stared at me in confusion. I covered the phone and whispered to her. "This nigga talmbout he gon kill me. Fuck this lame ass nigga."

Reecy put her hand on the phone and pulled it, but I pulled it back from her. "Lemme talk to this fuck nigga for a minute." I said.

Reecy exhaled and sat across from me. "Baby that's a pencil in your hand."

"What?" I screamed. "What you talmbout?"

Reecy stood up and snatched the phone from me, showing me it was a pencil. I passed out.

ICE

"I'm about to pull up to the grocery store now. You ready?" I asked Patron, one of my most loyal customers.

"I'm already here... same place as usual." He said with no hesitation.

"Aight bet, I'm like 3 minutes away." I said, and hung the phone up. I was driving up Cleveland Avenue, about to turn into the grocery store parking lot where he was at. As I drove, I thought about all of the items I'd sold him over the last couple years, and wondered what the hell he did with them. Every single time I saw him, he was wearing dirty clothes with his landscaping company logo patched on the shirt. If it wasn't for his consistency in wearing soiled clothing, I would have sworn up and down he was the damn police.

I turned into the parking lot and pulled up to his truck, where he was standing outside of it leaning against it. He was a tall dark-skinned man with un-groomed hair, and a rough looking beard. He smelled of gasoline, had oil on his hands, and green grass stains on the bottom of his jeans, which were much too big for him. His shoes were once white, but after cutting so much grass in them, they looked like they'd been dipped in a yellow-green stew, and baked in the sunlight. They were ugly.

I got out and put on a half smile. He smiled back, and when he did, I saw a load of potential with his perfect white teeth, and evenly dark skin. He even had a sparkle in his eye when he looked at me. I dismissed it however, because there was always a man with a sparkle in his eye when he looked at me. Hell, I just considered myself a normal chick, nothing special or different from the next.

People have constantly told me that I favored Bernice Burgos, although I begged to differ. That lady was perfect, and rich, and I was just a chick trying to make it in this cold world. After being raised by my abusive aunt, and seeing my mother and father in and out of jail and prison, and strung out on crack and heroin coming up, I didn't know sometimes if I was coming or going. I started stealing shit when I was 16 in order to escape my aunt's household. I ran away and never looked back the night she beat me with a mop stick for forgetting to mop the kitchen floor. I ran away from

Macon, GA six years ago and I never went back for any reason whatsoever.

When I first arrived in Atlanta all those years ago, I didn't know where to turn to, where I was going to stay, who I could ask for help, or even where my next meal was going to come from. It wasn't long before I befriended an older lady who went by the name of Ms. Lattis who helped me as best as she could. See Ms. Lattis was homeless also, but her reason was extremely different than most. She was a recovering crack addict who had fought hard to get her life back on the right track. She'd spent years clean and working as a secretary at an urgent care facility until the place shut down. She had an arrest record of being caught with user amounts of crack cocaine in the past, and that was enough to make her lose out on potential job positions. She ended up losing everything that she'd worked for, and on top of it all, she'd just discovered that she had diabetes.

No matter what she was going through back then, she still helped me as if she was perfectly healthy. She helped me become a woman. Taught me how to shoplift without ever getting caught, taught me things that only professional scammers would have in their arsenal, and became what I always needed in my life at the time… my backbone. I loved Ms. Lattis with everything in me.

I popped the trunk on my Porsche, opened a bag and looked in it. "Ok, I got these Rockstar jeans in here… They retail for $750, but hold on… lemme see how many pair I got…" I said as I counted the different colors I had. "You wear a size what? 36 right?" I asked without really expecting him to answer. From my experience I knew he wore a size 36, but it wouldn't matter if I gave him a size 34 or 38. He seemed not to care anyways since he never wore them.

I grabbed 5 pair of jeans out and 5 shirts. "Ok, these jeans and shirts would probably come up to around $3,500 or better in Lenox Mall, but you can just give me $1,400 and call it a night." I said as I turned around to face him. I moved a strand of hair out of my eye and watched him as he fidgeted in his pockets for the money. He never tried to talk me down, through all of the years I've done business with him, so instead of me over-charging him, I always made sure not to take advantage of his quietness.

His hand shook as he counted the money, and I started to feel sorry for him for some reason. I looked in the truck and saw that he had his Mexican friend with him, but he seemed to be minding his own business and wasn't paying any attention to us at all.

Patron continued counting his money silently, and judging by the way he always gave me an assortment of small bills– and by small bills I'm talking about fives, tens, twenties, and a lot of ones... I sometimes wondered if he was even able to afford to buy clothes so often. However, it really wasn't my duty to be inquiring about his personal affairs. It was only my goal to make some money and get out the way.

"Dang." He said silently. It was the first thing he'd said all night, and hearing him say anything with his surprisingly smooth voice made me nervous.

"Is everything ok?" I asked him, concerned.

He stared at me slightly embarrassed. "I'm sorry, just a moment." He replied back, and opened the door of his truck. I didn't want to be all in his business, so I walked back around to my driver-side door and had a seat in my Porsche.

PATRON

If I was a white boy, my face would have been flush-red. I didn't have enough to buy the clothes from her, and I really hated that. In my mind, Ice was my woman, and even though it wasn't realistic, I wanted to continue to support her hustle until it became reality. I lifted up my center console and pulled out the envelope that I'd put away to pay my rent with. I took a deep breath, and pulled half of the money out.

Jose turned and looked at me, but didn't say anything. I counted the difference that it required to buy all of the clothing, and put the envelope back in the console.

"Patron, you can just borrow the money from me amigo." Jose said as he started reaching in his pocket. I felt so bad about him offering. I mean after all, I'm the one who paid *his* salary.

"No, I'm fine Jose. I already have somebody that's going to buy the clothes from me later at double the price, so I'll make the money right back." He knew I was lying, but he didn't judge me, at least not to my face he didn't. I'd told him the same lie time and time again, and every time I told him the lie, he always just nodded at me.

"Besides, you need to send that money to Mexico to Suliz. We don't want her arguing with you again and getting on your case." I joked, smiling. Suliz was his wife, and we both knew she didn't play. He'd promised her that he was going to come to America and get established, and then send for her and the rest of the family, but with the way Donald Trump was tripping, Jose had switched his plans up to instead just stack as much money as he could to take care of his family back home.

"You're right my friend. You're right." Jose said and looked back out the window.

I took the money and closed the door on my truck. I walked back around to where Ice was and handed it to her. "Here is all of it." I handed it to her and looked away. I don't know why that woman made me so nervous after doing business with her for all of those years.

What made it so bad was I really liked that woman, but I was so intimidated by her that I knew I would never have the courage to tell her my true feelings. Every time I was away from her, I'd tell myself how I'm about to confess my love to her, and then as soon as I see her pull up in her beautiful vehicle, I would forget every word I rehearsed. I liked her terribly, but didn't know how she was ever supposed to know that without me telling her. It was that moment I decided I was going to at least flirt with her to let her know I'm interested.

It was then or never, I decided, and I was about to tell her something so sexy, that I knew she would be all over me from that moment on. I took a deep breath, and let her have it straight from the heart.

"These clothes are mighty sexy." I said, immediately regretting speaking. I was so stuck in a trance that my mind had gone absolutely blank. I didn't even know what I was talking about, and I certainly didn't want to talk again. I wrapped my arms around the clothes and walked back to my truck, my stomach hurting and my self esteem beaten with embarrassment. I tossed the clothes in the bed of the truck, and when I turned around, I saw Ice pull off in her vehicle with the quickness. I could tell that I'd scared the hell out of her, and knew I had ruined my chances on ever appearing "cool" in her eyes.

I wouldn't be surprised if I couldn't even buy clothes from her again after my behavior today. I sat in the truck and took a deep breath. I then had to figure out how I was going to get my rent money back up, since I'd just happily handed it away and it was due the next day. I frowned at my circumstances, yet knew that I would still have to press forward no matter what. I started the vehicle, and began driving in silence.

We got to Jose's stop and he reached his hand out towards me for a handshake. "I appreciate everything you do for me Patron." Jose said.

It was the same speech, and the same sentence he had been telling me for the past two years straight, and at that point, I knew he was genuinely appreciative of me giving him a chance to get money with me, but the truth of the matter was that I was probably happier about him taking a chance working with me than anything else.

"Hey Jose." I said as I shook his hand tightly. "Why do you tell me that every single time I drop you off?"

"Why? Because there's always a chance I may never see you again Patrick. You know I'm over here with no paperwork. I'm just doing my best trying to provide for my family and mind my business."

I figured as much, but I never mentioned anything about his routine until that moment. "You'll be fine Jose." I said. "Everything you were trying to do is going to work for you. You have a true friend in me." I meant everything I said to him.

I watched him hop out the truck and walk into the door of his apartment, locking it behind him. I shook my head and sent a silent prayer up for him. I didn't want him to ever be sent back to a place he didn't want to go. I wanted him to live peacefully, as he was simply a hard working Mexican trying to make a better life for himself and his family. It was moments like that, that made me hate Donald Trump and every thing he stood for. He was truly the lowest form of disgust that had ever combined to create a human being.

ICE

I have no idea why I jumped in my car so quick after doing business with Patron. He'd given an awkward compliment to the clothes I was selling him, and a part of me knew that he meant to give that compliment to me... And for some reason, I felt myself getting just as nervous with him as he was with me. That had never happened to me before, never in the entire time I've been doing business with him. Hell, that had never happened with me and anybody at all.

I dismissed the notion and continued my drive back to Buckhead, one of the most prestigious and expensive areas in Atlanta, GA. People saw me all the time driving a Porsche, getting money, dressed good and doing well, but they didn't really know much about me, and I wanted things that way. I hooked a left on Peachtree Street and followed the winding road through a seemingly endless valley of twists until I made it to Kingsdale Luxury Condos.

I'd been checking to make sure that nobody was following me, and when I was as sure as I was going to be, I took a left and went to the gated entrance of the community. I rolled my window down and quickly pressed my thumb against the fingerprint scanner followed by the pound key. The gate opened quickly, and I drove the Porsche inside of the location. There were Bentleys, Rolls Royces, Range Rovers, Maseratis, and Benzes parked everywhere. The landscaping was perfect, as if drawn by a master artist.

I thought about Patron and wondered how many years it would take him to get to this level in landscaping. It was the middle of Georgia, no ocean in range, and there were still endless rows of breathtaking palm trees, giving the place an exotic feel to it. I drove around the first set of apartments until I got to the Diamond Section, then I parked in the empty vacancy next to the beaten up Honda Accord with the cracked window shield.

That was my real car. More on this in a moment.

I swapped some of the leftover gear from the Porsche to the trunk of the Honda, and proceeded to walk up the steps of the luxurious complex. It was the first apartment complex I'd ever seen that had winding staircases outside of the residences. The handles were made of shiny gold, and there wasn't the first particle of trash anywhere in the vicinity. I walked one flight of stairs and walked down a glass hallway with television screens built into the walls and speakers in the ceiling, muted.

I stopped at apartment 218 and reached up to press the button, but before I could push it, the door opened. I stepped in, closed it quickly, and took a deep breath. "Hey Ms. Lattis." I said as the older lady smiled at me, showing all 10 of her remaining teeth.

"Hey Sugar." She said while walking towards the kitchen. "I made you something to eat. I know you been starving."

I don't know how she knew, but I was starving and didn't even realize how long I'd gone without eating. I obediently walked to the kitchen table and sat in a chair that was already pulled out.

"How did your day go Sugar?" Ms. Lattis asked while pulling a plate out of her cabinet.

"Uh... It was ok. We got a few diamond Rolexes and diamond bracelets out of Lenox today. It was a decent job, but I'm starting to get tired of the stores Ms. Lattis."

She turned around and frowned at me. "Sugar, what have I told you about that?"

"I know you always tell me that the stores are the safest way, but I really hate the fact that I gotta turn around and sell the products after the fact. I mean damn... I might as well sign up to be a wholesaler and open my own store at this point. I feel like I'm doing the same thing... Getting it for a little of nothing and selling it for a little profit." I confessed to Ms. Lattis. I'd been feeling like that a while, but every time I mentioned it, Ms. Lattis would convince me to stick with the stores.

"Baby it's not many options these days." Ms. Lattis said as she fixed my plate. She had her hair in a struggle bun, and I made a mental note to take her to get some extensions put in the first chance I got. "If you don't do stores, you gon' do time. I don't know how many times I gotta tell you that. You want some sweet tea? I got a new brand from Wal-Mart you gotta try. Hold on lemme' pour you a cup."

I shook my head and grinned as I watched the thin light-skinned woman rush to the refrigerator in excitement over her new sweet tea. I could tell that she was once a very beautiful woman in her younger years. Probably too beautiful... Seemed like she was the type of woman who were going to attract some of the most dangerous lions out of the jungle on any given day.

"Sugar just because you're tired of stealing out the stores doesn't mean you go do something else. In fact, it may be time for you to just hang it up for a while. I mean... I don't know why you're working so hard anyways. I don't need all this fancy stuff you done bought me. I can drive your Honda, I don't need no Porsche. I can live in the hood, I don't need to be way out here with these boujee ass folks."

"Nah, you deserve to live here Ma." I caught myself and took a deep breath. Whenever I got emotional, I always called her Ma, but she didn't like that because she didn't like the way my real mother treated me, and didn't want to be thought of in the same light.

"You know I'm nothing like your mama." Ms. Lattis said, getting offended again.

"I'm sorry, it just crept out. I didn't mean nothing by it. What I was saying though... you deserve to stay out here and live like this more than anybody who lives out here. If it wasn't for you teaching me the game, I'd be in jail or prison like the other boosters who didn't have a genius to teach them how to do it the right way. I never even knew this could be a legitimate profession until you taught me."

"Yea but... that's still not enough for me to drive the car you worked for and stay in the place you put all your hard work in for. I say take a break and downgrade me all the way around the board. Stack your money and let's fall below the radar for a while." Ms. Lattis said as she sat the plate down in front of me and put a cup beside it.

I picked the cup up and tried the tea that she was raving so much about. Surprisingly it was pretty good. I smiled and sat the cup down, and matched her gaze as she stood over me smiling at me. I swallowed because I knew that she knew what I was thinking. She seemed to always be able to read me well.

"Baby don't worry about my health condition. I'm going to make it through. I'ma be good. I haven't had any issues in a long time, so we can't use that as an excuse."

"Ms. Lattis I wanna hit a bank one time. Or even an armored truck. Hell I need some things in my life that's going to bring me money at a faster pace. I don't wanna have to sell my merchandise every time I steal it. That's how I've been getting cheated out of my money, because I have to rely on sneaky ass Reecy Pooh to bring me my cut. But that's not my main concern. At the end of the day, I'm in my early 20s, and I just need excitement."

"Sugar if you need excitement, why don't you go to Six Flags over Georgia?" Ms. Lattis asked with a serious look on her face.

"And you need to make up your mind. One day she's your best friend, one day she's sneaky ass Reecy Pooh. Listen dear... I'm telling you what I know... just stick with the stores. Any of those other situations are going to either get you killed or sent to prison for a very long time."

"But Ms. Lattis you did it." I said in a pleading tone.

"I was young, dumb, and stupid Ice, and I didn't have any guidance or anybody to teach me otherwise. I could have easily gotten killed in those situations, and I've regretted that I pulled such a stunt on many occasions."

I wasn't trying to hear it, but I didn't want to argue with her. I bit my tongue. Well I tried to. "Ms. Lattis you got away with a million dollars cash! I want a lick like that. Damn. Just one! That's really a story only a legend can re-tell." I said as I smile at her in amazement.

"Again... I was young and stupid. On top of that, I had to split the money with the people who were with me on the job. And another thing... It was hard as hell to trust people back then, so where in the hell would you find loyal people at like that this these days? You might as well give it up. Then... I never told you this... but it was after that particular job that I started doing drugs."

A headache seemed to be forming out of the blue. She'd never told me this part of the story before, and I didn't know if she was adding it on just to discourage me, or if she was telling me to truth.

"What happened Ms. Lattis?" As I was asking her the question, my phone started vibrating. I picked it up looked at the screen, turned it back off and put it back in my pocket.

"Maybe another day I'll tell you about it sugar. As of right now, it's a lot of things regarding that situation that I just can't discuss."

I shook my head and drank more of the tea. I know she was a hell of a thief, because she'd taught me, but for some reason I couldn't picture her being a robber of any sort. She just had too much finesse for me to picture her snatching some shit. Me on the other hand... I had a growing urge in me to start swiping shit out of people's hands, as finessing was becoming to bore and drain me.

I stood up and sat the keys to the Porsche on the table. "Where are my keys to the Honda?" I asked, stepping back from the table.

"Why don't you just drive the Porsche sugar? I'll keep the Honda."

"I only use the Porsche to sell my clothes and stuff. I don't have any other reason for it than that. If I pull up in a Honda and try to sell clothes, they'll think I'm struggling, won't believe the stuff is legit, and they won't buy it. But when I pull up in your Porsche, all that shit is just as good as sold."

"More of the reason you need to keep the Porsche Ice. That's your image that you built."

"I want you to have it." I said and walked away from her. I walked to the counter top and grabbed her purse, reached in and got my keys out. I turned to face her and she was standing with her arms folded. I walked up to her and gave her a quick hug.

"I'm about to head to my place Ms. Lattis. Everything is going to be alright. I'll see you tomorrow." I said, staring in her eyes.

"Why are you doing all this?" She said, tears forming in her eyes. You got me living all fancy, meanwhile you're living in the trap? Driving a beaten up car? What is this all about? You're going to have to let me know what's going on with you or I'm just going to not accept any of it anymore!"

I took a deep breath and shook my head. "Ms. Lattis, you have no idea the hell I was going through when you saved me those years ago. I'm not doing this completely for you, because I stash away money all the time, but I know that it's no way I could ever re-pay you for all the blessings you've bestowed upon me. You did more for me than anybody has ever done for me, and in return I just do the best I can to show you that I really love and care for you.

You helped me get off of the streets when I was 16 and lost. You helped me perfect my craft, and taught me things that only my real mother would have been able to taught me had she gave a fuck." And as I said those words, the tears started flowing. I was having a difficult time expressing myself to a woman who hated for me to show emotion. She always told me that as long as I was in the streets, I was never to show what I cared about because it would always be used against me later. I understood what she meant, but I could never understand what it had to do with me and her.

"I know you don't care to hear this Ms. Lattis, but you're like a mother to me. I take that back... You're like a mother, sister, aunt, and a best friend. It's your words and advice I seek when I'm down or when I'm lost. It's your presence I seek when I'm fine and nothing's wrong at all. You are a vital part of my life, and as long as I'm getting money, you have to let me look out for you the way I want to."

Ms. Lattis took a deep breath and put a half smirk on her face. She didn't immediately reply, instead she wrapped her arms around me and gave me a longer hug.

"Alright then sugar. But you be safe out there in them streets, you hear? And if you ever need me to do a job with you, then you come get me and let me know what it is we're doing. I know you have mixed emotions about Reecy Pooh sometimes, so if you ever need a veteran on the job, I'm here ready and able. I may be 54 years old, but I can move and groove with the best of the best in these streets."

I laughed at her choice of words. "Move and groove though? O.K. I'll keep that in mind, but I can tell you right now that that day will never come. You're going to stay in retirement while I run this check up for us. I'll see you tomorrow." I said as I walked out of the apartment.

If only I'd understood the power of that conversation, and the effect it would have over my future.

REECY POOH

"Shit nigga what the fuck! You ok?" I screamed after seeing Rhondo pass out in the wheelchair.

I put my hand on his neck to see if he was dead or alive, and when I felt a pulse, I knew I would have to put that nigga in the hospital. I didn't know if I had what it took to take care of a grown man suffering from bullet wounds, and having to teach him how to read, write, and do basic shit all over again.

"Shit! This shit is nerve racking." I closed my eyes and dialed 911. I put it on speakerphone while I pulled his head up from him laying in that awkward ass position. I knew that if I didn't, he was going to be in severe pain later when he woke up.

"911 what's your emergency?"

"Hey. My boyfriend got shot a while—"

"What's your address? I'm about to dispatch officers and an ambulance right now."

"Wait, no... He didn't just get shot."

"Ok, what's your emergency?"
"Bitch hang that phone up. Dumb ass bitch." His words startled me.

I looked at Rhondo and he was staring at me like I was the scum of the earth. I just didn't understand why he hated me so much, when all I'd ever done was try to help his ass. I was so tired of his shit.

"Why the fuck you keep on calling me out my name nigga?" I screamed on him. He was in a wheelchair so it wasn't like he could do shit to me. But instead of me slapping the shit out of him, I left it alone. It was what it was. Fuck him.

"Is everything ok?" The 911 dispatcher asked.

"Yes, all is fine." I answered and hung the phone up.

I stared at Rhondo with venom in my eyes. All I was trying to do was make sure he was straight and he was just so dead set on figuring out how to embarrass me by all means. I looked down at his pants and saw that he'd peed on himself. It wasn't there when I came in the house, so he must have peed himself when he passed out.

"Aye look... let me take you to the bathroom and wash you up. Will you be able to help me—"

"Nah fuck that. Just let me get some sleep." He said with bitterness in his voice.

What the fuck did I do to this nigga for him to hate me so much?

I couldn't wait until he healed so I can leave his ass standing on his own two feet. I couldn't afford the karma of leaving him while he was down in a wheelchair. I can afford the rest of the shit though. He just didn't know.

"Nigga you got piss on your clothes and you don't want me to clean you up? You'd rather lay in piss? You don't wanna be clean?"

"Bitch just gimme a Percocet."

"Wow. Bitch just gimme a Percocet. That's just how your dirty ass operate in these fuckin streets too. You be dirty as fuck, knowing you know better, but all you need is something to numb your fucking pain. Weed, pills, drank, alcohol, all that shit... you just a fine ass dirty ass fiend out here. Got me out here looking stupid as fuck. Nigga fuck you!" I screamed at him.

I grabbed the bottle of Percocets off of the counter. "Here you want a fuckin pill nigga? Fine!" I untwist the top and tossed the bottle of pills in his lap.

"You say you just wanna lay down? Say no got damn more lame ass nigga!"
I pushed his wheelchair into the bedroom, and stopped when it was right by the bed. I walked out of the bedroom, went into the bathroom and stood in front of the mirror. I turned the faucet on in the sink, but it was no match for the faucet on my face. Tears shredded my makeup, and it hurt my feelings that I was settling for a no good ass nigga who didn't give a fuck about how he talked to me or treated me. I was beginning to actually hate that

nigga, as he had no idea the level of resentment that was beginning to grow inside of me.

I wiped my tears and took a deep breath. I wasn't about to go for that shit that night. Fuck that. I grabbed my phone and called Jiip for a couple of reasons. One of those reasons *had* to go right, I *needed* one of them to go right.

"Yah." He answered nonchalantly.

"Aye bruh, what's up?" I asked, listening to the background trying to figure out where I thought he could be.

"Shit you know what's up. I'm bout to get this damn money." He said in his signature deep ragged voice. He had a voice that reminded me of a cross between DMX and Scarface, the rapper. He kind of looked like a cross between Scarface and DMX too.

"Well shit... you think I'll be able to see you tonight? Or what?" I tapped my fingers against the counter top while awaiting a response.

"Damn. You getting out late night? You must be finally leaving your nigga or something?" He said with amusement in his voice.

"Nigga what's it gon be? I'm not about to play with you Jiip. Either you gon see me or you ain't. You gon' have the money for me? What's up nigga? If you ain't say you ain't so I can find me something else to fuckin do."

"Damn lil mama calm yo' lil' midget ass up. You ain't but 4 foot 7 talking all that shit."

"I'm 4'11" thank you. But let me know what the fuck we doing."

He sighed, and let out a moan as if he was exhausted. "Yea... shit just meet me at the spot in two hours. I'll be done with shit on my end by then and I should be back. If I ain't at the spot in two hours, drive to the other side of the street and wait on me."

"The other side of the street? Why?" I asked with a frown on my face.

"Shit because you never know what can go wrong during my missions. So if the police were to come search my shit, you don't need to be just sitting there looking crazy.

I smiled. That was the type of shit that turned me on. A nigga who even remotely acted like he gave a fuck about me and my well-being. Despite his brashness and abrasive street nigga mentality, he always showed me that he was thinking of my safety when he dealt with me. That was the shit that made my panties wet. It was a hidden gem in street niggaz, and a bitch like me knew how to locate that shit when it existed.

I hung the phone up, blushing from ear to ear.

"2 hours I'ma be there nigga." I said while staring at my smiling reflection in the mirror. I'd cheered up, and just that quick my entire mood was better.

RHONDO

"I like that ring right there in the middle."

"The one with the canary diamond? This one?" The salesperson asked as she placed her fingers on the ring.

"No the one right beside it. The one with the white princess cut diamonds in the shape of a heart, with the solitaire diamond in the middle. That shit super hard. I want that one." I said, knowing Reecy Pooh was going to love it.

I was gon' finally propose to her ass and clean my act up. She'd been by my side for so long, through all of my bullshit days, and I didn't want her to think that she'd done it all for nothing. I truly loved her ass, and I was going to show her that I cared. I was going to finally propose.

I thought about all the times I fucked up the money I owed the plug, all the losses I took in the streets, having to flush the dope, sometimes getting on high speed chases and tossing the dope in the bushes... All the shit I went through in the streets from having workers getting arrested with the work, and me always being able to bounce back because of Reecy Pooh. She deserved this and more.

The salesperson picked the ring up and placed it in my hand. "You like this one?"

"Fuckin right. I love this one. Shit what's the ticket on it?"

She took the ring out of my hand and pulled the ticket out of the inside. She grabbed the calculator and typed some numbers in.

"This one retails for $76,000, but I can give it to you for $40,000. That's a huge discount."

"Shit but it ain't huge enough. Got damn that muthafucka must come with a car? Let's look at the other ring then. Matter fact, let's look at the one on the bottom with just the one diamond on it." I pointed to the bottom left corner.

The salesperson picked the ring up and looked at the ticket. She typed on the calculator and turned to face me. "This one I can let you get it for $4,000."

That was more my lane. "Hell yea. Shit I'ma put it on layaway today. I'ma give you $200 to hold it." I said as I started reaching in my pocket.

"Sir, we require at least 20% to hold items on layaway, and it's non-refundable."

"20%? How much is that? I said, quickly trying to calculate the amount I'd have to give her."

"It'll be $800 to hold it."

I took a deep breath. Reecy Pooh betta be happy bout this damn ring I was bout to get her ass. I ain't have no money to waste on no bullshit like that, but shit... fuck it. All these chicks that ride with they nigga, all they want is to be able to show off a wedding, and show off two rings– engagement ring and the wedding ring. They didn't give a fuck about the rest of the shit. Niggas stay cheating, keep fuckin other hoes, keep having kids, man the shit never stopped just because of the ceremony.

But I understood. It was just like how niggaz wanna be seen as the man, or how certain things niggaz do make it seem like some type of rite of passage... Like threesomes... shit every street nigga has either had a threesome, or lied about having a damn threesome. Probably 85% of these niggaz be lying though.

So yea, I think threesomes to a nigga is the same thing as what getting married is to a chick. Because after the threesome is over with, nothing changes with your life. You go back to doing the same shit. You don't become superman, and you don't win a trophy. It's just some more shit to talk about.

I gave the lady the $800 to hold the ring, and she gave me a receipt to bring back for when it was time for me to pick it up. I walked out of the shop feeling like I'd done something great for a change. I'd fucked up so many times... and for once I was making the right move for my relationship.

I got outside and climbed in my Escalade. I called my homeboy Stats, but I didn't get an answer. I was tryna see how much work he had left. I dropped him off a quarter key the day before and needed him to go head and get that off. My trap was moving slow, and I didn't know if it was due to a better product or if somebody was stealing my clientele. I was going to get to the bottom of the shit though.

My phone rang and I seen my baby mama's name pop up. I hit the end button. I ain't wanna talk to her, I needed to find out what's up with my money. I called Stat's phone again and it went to voicemail. My phone rang again.

"Man what the fuck you want bitch?" I asked Lisa's crazy ass.

"Stupid ass fuck nigga your got damn son asked about you ol' stupid ass nigga. You too busy with your head up Reecy Pooh's stankin ass to even pay attention to your own child. You a real fuck boy for real!"

"Bitch quit hitting my fuckin phone before you get blocked dumb ass bitch. If you need some money let me know and I'll get it, otherwise get yo' ratchet ass off my line."

"No nigga. Yo son needs time! Time not fuckin money! He's 9 years old and he wants to spend time with his no good ass Daddy."

"Tell lil man I'm going to pick him up after I leave the gym today."

"No nigga, I told him you were working, and that you'll reach out to him when you wanna get him. I'm not telling him shit else regarding you. You not about to make me lie to him for you. You know where we live, so you bring your ass here and explain yourself."

"Put him on the phone."

"Nigga fuck no. Pull up! Your car ain't broke."

I was tired of her ass. She was really getting on my damn nerves. I was about to reply, but I didn't have the energy. I hung up on her and turned my phone off. I was going to stop by their house later to see them. I knew her real issue was that she needed some dick. It was 2017, and she wasn't fooling nobody.

The new "I want some dick" phrase was "Your son wants to see you." Every street nigga knew this, and knew that if he didn't want his baby mama doing the fuckin most, they would have to fuck they ass every once in a while whether he wanted to or didn't want to. It came with the territory.

I was backed my truck up, getting ready to head to the gym to release some of my steam. In the past when I argued with her ass it always made me angry, but I'd found out that instead of me being in a bad mood for days at a time, all I had to do was hit the gym and get that stress away from me.

I turned around, to make sure I didn't hit anybody's car while backing up outside of the jewelry store, and after I'd backed up enough, I reached up to put my car in gear to go forward.

Pop! I heard a firecracker go off in front of me, and turned around to see what was going on.

As soon as my face faced the windshield, the windshield disappeared.

Pop! Pop! I ducked down low, no longer caring if my truck ran into a car. I didn't know what was going on but that it wasn't good.

My driver's side window shattered and my door opened up. "You know what it is fuck nigga!" A voice yelled from above me.

I was really confused. I'd never been robbed before, and then it being in broad daylight was really fuckin with my mentally. It was like I was dreaming, as if it wasn't really happening.

"Give it up nigga! Don't play stupid!"

"Give what up?"

I probably shouldn't have said that.

Pop! Pop! Pop! Pop. It felt like a tattoo artist was taking his needle and stabbing me all over the place. The pain, the sound of the bullet shell exploding, the smell of gunpowder, the memory of me not being able to move, being thrown to the ground, the sound of footsteps against the grass, the sound of the tire turning against the rocks, the exhaust, the screaming of bystanders, the puddle of blood I was laying in, the memory of dirt going in my nose and me not being able to get up off of the ground.

***

I woke up in my wheelchair sweating. I'd been having the exact same dream over and over since being shot. When I got to the hospital, I made sure to tell my baby mama not to bring my son up there. Whoever was trying to kill me didn't finish the job, and I definitely didn't want them to hurt my son being that they couldn't get me. I'd been running the streets and doing so much dirt that I had no idea who was trying to kill me or why they wanted me dead.

Waking up in the hospital, the only person I wanted by my side was my savage ass girlfriend, Reecy Pooh. She was from the streets, so she already knew what could be expected. She knew to bring her heat, and she knew not to talk to no cops about shit. She was the only woman I ever needed.

Waking up in the bedroom however, I was alone.

There was no Reecy Pooh, and since I got shot, the vibe I got from her was nothing like how it was before me getting shot. It was almost like she was disappointed that I was still living after going through my ordeal. It was in her face, and her tone when she said certain things.

I heard her on the phone with someone earlier, but I didn't know who it was, nor was I going to ask her and get in her business. It was what it was. I really needed Stats to call me though. The last time I talked to him was at the hospital, when he brought me the money from selling that work. I hadn't seen him since, and he hadn't even hit me to check on me.

That's just the life of a street nigga though. Too busy for the basics, always chasing that next dollar, that life I just knew it all too much.

I was dozing back off to sleep when my phone lit up, I grinned when I saw Stats' name on the caller ID.

Jiip

I didn't have time to waste when it came to hitting licks. I was that nigga in the A when it came strong arm snatching shit. Pistol whippin, rope tying, kick a do' wide the hell open with the bottom of my sneakers, I was with all that shit. If a nigga saw my face in Atlanta, and I was taking something from him, he wasn't gon' live to tell a got damn soul. That's just how I rolled. I been knocking niggaz off and taking shit ever since I was 17 years old. Shit was never gon change with me, that's what I was put on this earth to do. Just how snakes was put on earth to snatch a life, so was I.

"Where you think you goin' nigga?" I asked Albert. He had a mask in one hand and a pistol in the other.

"Shit you said we had to hit a lick..." Albert said, looking up at me wide-eyed. He was the same age I was when I first started hitting licks, and he was getting better and better by going on jobs with me.

"Nigga put that mask up. Get you another gun out the closet and bring your ass on. You gon' be on driver duty tonight."

"Driver duty?" Albert whined. "Why can't I go in the spot with you? You said I did a good job of having your back last time Unc."

"Nigga you got my back in the car tonight. Tonight I'm going in barefaced. The last time I went in a spot barefaced, you damn near threw up your DNA all in the got damned house. You never seen a bitch get her brains blowed out before? What's up? You wanna see this shit again?"

"Oh nah, I'll drive then." Albert said, frowning up at the thought of the massacre.

"I know damn well you will drive nigga. It's been a minute since I had some shit on the news, and I gotta make my presence be felt again out here in the streets. Niggaz was sleeping on me... Talking about it's some West Side ass nigga out there in the streets colder than me. Ain't nobody fuckin with me!"

Albert swallowed hard and went to the back to grab another gun.

"Gon head and use the bathroom while you're back there! I can't afford for you to have a weak ass stomach if I come out the house with blood all over my body. I need you to drive like a professional, no matter what the car smells like."

***

We were on our way to Decatur when we saw some niggaz in a parking lot crowded around a nigga who looked like he was dancing.

"Wait what the fuck? Pull over!" I instructed Albert.

He glanced at me with a confused look on his face.

"Man pull the got damn car over into that parking lot!"

Albert frowned and took a deep breath.

"Something wrong nigga?" I asked while staring at him like he was crazy.

"Nah... But shit we can't rob all them niggaz. It's just two of us, how the hell we gon' get away if all them niggaz is strapped?" He was pissing me off, and I had the strong urge to knock his top row of teeth out, but suddenly I had a better plan for his ass.

I pulled the Draco AK 47 out of my backpack and sat it in my lap, not saying another word. Just that quickly, I'd come up with a nice ass plan.

"Is this close enough?" Albert asked as he parked close to the crowd surrounding the rapper.

"Yep, perfect." I grabbed the automatic gun, and jumped out of the car. I started walking towards the crowd, and the closer I got, the better I could hear what the rapper was saying.

"Whole lotta gang shit nigga! You see us out here nigga! In the hood, on Instagram Live nigga. Who the fuck fucking with us? Gang shit, gang shit, whole lotta gang shit bitch! All you fuckin rappers talking all that talk, don't ever let me see you out here nigga. Look at my neck ho. $100,000 on my neck, another 40 on my wrist, and you know we keep $100,000 in cash on us at all times nigga. Fuck you mean nigga! All y'all social media gangstas betters watch your fuckin mouth when you speak our names. You see how we rocking! 100 round drums on the Dracos bitch!"

Then there was an awkward silence as they all turned the phones off. "All y'all phones off?" The rapper asked his crew.

"Yea they off."

"Play it back lemme see what it look like on video." The rapper said as they all crowded around a cell phone.

That was my cue. "Excuse me bro. How you?" I asked, as loud as possible.

The crowd stared at me like I was bothering them, and they turned back to look at the cell phone. I walked closer to the crowd until I was right in front of them all. "Excuse me." I said again.

The rapper spoke up. "Somebody give this bum ass nigga $1 so he can get the fuck away from me."

His words shocked me, and it was even more shocking when one of his do-boys reached into the backpack right in front of me to retrieve a dollar bill. I knew they wasn't street niggaz, because if they were, they would know to never underestimate any human being when you were unable to see that human being's other hand.

I swung my Draco around like a carousel and fired some shots in the air. *Tott- Tott-Tott-Tott.*

Judging by the way they started ducking and hitting the ground in fear, their reaction told me that their gun couldn't have been real. These fools ain't never been around a real Draco in their whole life. A whole group of young niggaz in spandex clothes and pink and purple dreadlocks talking shit for the internet about other niggaz who talk shit for the internet. I wasn't knocking them, but I had a job to do just like they did.

"Gimme those chains, that watch, and that bag of money nigga. Give it up fuck nigga!" I screamed while pointing the gun at his head.

"They're not real!" He screamed.

"What's not real nigga?"

"None of it."

"What?" I screamed. I was pissed at that point. "Give it to me anyway fuck nigga! I oughta blow your muthafuckin brains out for flexin! Gimme your fuckin phone too ol' bitch ass nigga! Give it to me!"

He did as I said, and handed me fake custom jewelry, a bag of "motion picture use only" movie money, a fake Rolex, and his cell phone.

"Why is your screen cracked nigga?" I yelled at his broke ass.

"I-I-I... Please.... Please don't.... P-P-Pleaseee don't.... Please..." I slapped him in the face with the back of my hand, and then flipped my hand back around and slapped him with my open palm.

"Don't you ever get your dumb ass out here flexing again about a Draco, or about some money, and you damned sure bet' not post anything about no jewelry again for the rest of your career. Get this straight... You and your whole crew... Y'all some straight bitches my nigga. Real hoes. Real Spongebob Square Pants ass lames! How the fuck you get robbed for your fake shit plus your cell phone? Y'all fuckin' me up from doing *my* got damn job."

I shook my head, pissed off at the young ass bums. I should have known though, all niggaz is doing these days is flexing for the internet and telling on them selves. Shit I had an Instagram page, but the only picture I had ever posted was of the ground. Just a reminder to these niggas that that's where I was sending that ass. I only had Instagram to catch licks, I could never be a lick.

I walked backwards with their items in my other hand. "Stop fuckin' lookin at me!" I screamed and let some more shots off in the air. I turned, jumped in the car and Albert hit the gas.

As we made it a couple of blocks away from the rappers, Albert cracked a smile on his face. "Yoooo that was lit Unc!" He laughed. "How did you know them niggaz wasn't strapped for real? That was some brave shit!"

"Strapped with what? Haha, these niggaz is clowns these days. Anytime I see a crowd of niggaz and a camera, I'm robbing that ass from here on out. These niggaz is pussy!"

Albert kept driving and hopped on the expressway headed to Decatur. I connected my phone via bluetooth and played a song called "Hustlin" by Young Scooter, YFN Lucci, and Meek Mill. I inhaled the vibe of the song while rubbing my Draco like a puppy. I was so in love with my guns, so enthusiastic about taking a life... The average person would probably say something was wrong with me, but I could say the same thing about the average person. The same way that some people eat and breathe music, or lived and loved sports, I felt the same way about taking shit. If they were to put together an All-Star team for robbers and life snatchers, I would be the starting point guard.

We made it to the location in no time. Or maybe it seemed that way because I was zoned out through the duration of the trip. All I was thinking about was the task at hand. It was about to be a nasty one, one that was going to send shock waves through the community, but one that just had no other option but to get done. It was time for it.

"Albert, just relax and don't panic. If you see some crazy shit that looks like I absolutely have to abort mission, just blow the fuck out of the horn. If it's a police situation, you already know how we rolling... Right?"

Albert nodded his head in agreement. We'd done this several times, so he was accustomed to the procedure at that point. The house we'd pulled up to was an older wooden house in what looked to be a quiet neighborhood. I closed my eyes for a split second, knowing that this quietness would all change tomorrow. I stepped out of the car and closed the door lightly.

Once out of the car with a weapon, there was no time to wait, and no more time to hesitate. That's how other people got caught and ended up dead or going to prison later. Hesitation didn't exist with me. I never spared shit on a mission like this. I ran straight up to the door, pausing only to smirk at the welcome mat that read, "If you're not God, take your shoes off."

I picked my shoes up off of the ground and kicked them muthafuckas against the door, one kick broke the locks off that bitch. I ran in and instantly recognized the layout of the house. I studied house plans every day from architecture websites so that once I was in there, I always knew how to locate the master bedroom. I didn't need to case shit out. This house plan was a Bassett, a basic 3 bedroom-3 bathroom spot.

I ran to the master bedroom and flipped on the light, where an older lady was laying there snoring away. She was exactly who I expected to see, and sleeping exactly how I was expecting her to be. The older lady was Block Sushi's mama, a nigga who'd been moving a decent amount of dope in Atlanta. He wasn't on no kingpin status, but he definitely had been flexing heavy buying big boy VIP sections in the club and shit.

I went to the closet where I was told the safe was going to be. I got the drop on the situation from a nigga who was once close to Block Sushi, but something had happened between them to make the nigga turn on him. Needless to say I got the info from him and buried his ass the same night he gave me the info. Fuck that nigga, I won't let him turn on me... He can turn in his grave.

I grabbed the safe and listened to the old lady snore. I could have easily just walked out of the house and let her sleep peacefully. She was sleeping so hard... It must have been her routine for many years because she never woke up for any sound or any suspicion. I knew I could be clean about the situation, let her live and have one less problem on my hands. I mean... shit... what did she do to deserve to die? I had no answer to that. I got to the door and thought about letting her live, and suddenly the thought disappeared.

I pulled out my Draco and lit her muthafuckin ass up while she was sleeping.

Tot-tot-tot-tot-tot-tot-tot-tot-tot-tot-tot-tot.

12 shots in rapid succession. I felt nothing... No emotion... No hurt, no pain, no remose... Just happiness. I ran out the house and jumped into the waiting car. Albert took off. We hit the highway, and disappeared into the Atlanta moonlight. Nothing made me feel better than my sick hobby. For some reason I felt like I was connecting with spirits when I killed someone. I felt as if I'd done a good deed... Maybe not a good deed according to society's beliefs, but in another realm, I felt like I was helping to put the puzzle pieces together; helping to create angels for those who needed them on this cold planet.

One love.

ICE

I got in my Honda and dialed Reecy's number. I put my seatbelt on and cracked a window while waiting on her to answer.

"Hey boo thang!" Reecy said happily.

I was glad she was in a better mood with all of the drama she'd been going through dealing with Rhondo.

"Hey Reecy Babi!" I laughed. Sometimes she really was my best friend, and sometimes I didn't know who she was, but I guess the streets of Atlanta was so vicious that it could disfigure your personality sometimes.

"Did you see your usual client?" Reecy asked. For a moment I didn't even know what she was talking about.

"My client? I'm just leaving Ms. Lattis' house."

"No... the dude... Patrick... Patron, whatever his name is."

"Ohhhh yea. I saw Pat, he looked out for me. I got a little money for you out of it if you haven't gotten off the jewelry yet." I said, fishing for info. I really needed her to have already sold that shit.

"Yea... I'm going to need it Ice."

"Damn, I thought you said earlier the nigga had $40,000 for you?" I said nervously. I had bills coming up, and $20,000 was barely going to cut it. If I couldn't get the $20k I'd be really in a bad position with my bills and Ms. Lattis' medical bills. I needed my cut, bad.

"Yea he's supposed to be giving it to me tonight. I'm going to spend the night at his spot and I'll see you in the morning with the money... So just keep my cut from the clothes, and I'll just take it out of your cut of the money." Reecy Pooh said hesitantly.

"You ok girl? Shit I don't mind coming wherever the hell you're at to get my cut tonight. That way I can get up early in the morning to pay Ms. Lattis' medical bills. You know I'm two months behind on her rent and the Porsche payments because we didn't work last month since the situation came up with your man getting shot up."

I was trying to get my damn money. I didn't have time to waste. The past few weeks all we'd managed to do was get clothes, purses, shoes and shit. This was the first good lick we'd had in a long time, and I needed to be paid for my role in the shit.

"Ice I ain't going nowhere between tonight and in the morning. It's only a few hours away baby. Right now it's midnight. I'll call you in the morning as soon as I get up. Everything's going to be ok." Reecy Pooh sounded so reassuring, but I wasn't convinced. However, I didn't want to make it seem like I didn't trust her, because then she really might do some crazy shit for real.

"O.K. Reecy Pooh. Well I'm about to get me some rest, so I'll see you tomorrow." I lied.

"Bitch you ain't about to rest!" She knew me too well. "Yo' ass about to go probably put some more research together."

I laughed. I couldn't even deny her accusations. "Well goodnight Reecy Pooh... Be careful out there..."

"You too Ice Ice Babi." She said and laughed.

***

I lived in the hood in Jonesboro, in a low income complex by the name of Keystone Apartments. My bills weren't major, and I didn't care for the shine, or to be recognized in the streets. All I cared about was taking care of the lady who took care of me when she didn't have to, and being able to save up money without ever having to touch it until I was older in age. I had a stash of money that I never touched. If I wasn't able to come up with money to pay a bill, that stash was never to be touched. I had the utmost in discipline for it because I know there was no retirement plan for a booster. I had to put my own 501k program together, and it was definitely together.

When I parked my Honda, I saw police taping off an area about a half block or so down the street, and I was guessing that someone got shot like usual. I was dumb to the struggle, numb to the streets, and certainly numb to the activities that took place on the daily basis. I locked the door on my beat up Honda and walked up to my apartment door. I saw some new scratches beside the lock and figured that someone must have tried to break in while I was gone. It was an unsuccessful attempt, and it was humorous because people had been trying to break into my apartment for an entire year straight with no luck on figuring it out.

Someone apparently thought I had money hidden in my apartment. I really needed whatever was giving them so much consistent confidence in me to give me that same level of faith also. I unlocked my door and placed my thumb on the hidden fingerprint reader in the right side of the door frame. All of the locks popped open and allowed me access to my apartment. Even though I lived in the hood, the inside of my place was nice and modern. It was clean and it smelled good, but that's about it.

I still lived in the hood, and still had the same problems that other people in the hood had. No matter what I did for pest control, I still had roaches seeping in my house from other people's places. The new 2017 roaches didn't give a fuck about no pest control. They were immune to the shit at this point.

I locked the door and went to my bedroom to begin my research and studying for the night. On the wall I had a vision board that I fully planned on following all the way. My vision board was awkward as hell, and it was why I never ever showed it to anybody. Some of the items I'd attached to the board included a ski mask, a Brinks truck, an automatic rifle, a getaway car, and the cast from Set It Off.

I was so intrigued by the next level of boosting... actually putting together licks big enough so that I could eat for longer periods of time that it had became an obsession of mine. Every night I came home and studied YouTube for bank heists gone wrong and armored truck robberies gone bad, and it seemed like the worse two things that can go wrong is either being killed for being sloppy, or ending up on a high speed chase... also a result of being sloppy.

I couldn't see a seasoned criminal like myself ending up in any of those scenarios. Of course I couldn't do it alone though. I would need Reecy Pooh to hear me out one time in order to pull one of these off. I know it would go way better if I had a larger circle of friends and people that were down, but that just wasn't my reality. I had one down bitch who I felt I could trust through some shit like that, but every time I tried bringing that up to her, she would always say that it was a man's sport.
I believed otherwise.

I pulled a new armored truck robbery gone bad video up, this time one that took place in London, since I'd already studied every single video I could find from the United States. I turned the volume down and ran the video through an app so that it would run in slo-mo. While it ran in slow motion, I took the time to critique the techniques used by the would-be robbers based on every mistake I seen them make. In 30 seconds I spotted 4 different mistakes, and about 15 seconds later, one of the men were dead, and the other one managed to jump in the car and take off.

A few minutes later he was in a high-speed chase with the police, something that he was unable to avoid. I thought for a second and wrote down a new topic on my study sheet:

Avoiding high-speed chases by Investing:

A) It is my opinion that people don't invest the money or utilize their resources to learn how circumvent certain situations. If I'm going to pull off such a robbery of great proportions, then I'm also going to invest in the situation appropriately. Tomorrow I need to find a custom car shop. I feel like my getaway vehicle should be able to change colors at the touch of a button. If I'm going to steal a million dollars, I should be willing to invest $20,000 into making myself have a legit chance.

B) The same way the car should be able to change colors, I should not be easily identifiable as a black suspect. I should have a makeup artist to perfect me as a white woman. There is no excuse for not investing in these alterations to give myself the best chance of success. Once I get away, I should be able to eliminate the color of my skin just as I eliminate the color of the car. The car should also have stash spots that will not be simple to locate.

I finished writing and added this new section to my notebook, which at that point was about 200 pages long, and filled with ideas that were both genius and terrible ones. One day I knew I was going to make my dream happen, but until then I was going to perfect it on paper first.

I turned the computer off and went into the kitchen. I grabbed a Solo Cup and filled it with ice. I had a fresh bottle of Patron Silver on the countertop. I popped the seal and poured it across the ice. Quickly my mind flashed back to Patrick, and wondered why he called himself Patron. I wondered if he drank Patron also, and if he had a girlfriend who drank with him or if he drank alone. As I took a few sips I started to wonder if he could make me feel as good as this cup made me feel, and if it would last longer or make my body levitate the same way.

I touched myself for a minute, and then I came to my senses. I snapped out of my crazy fantasy and went and washed my hands. *I didn't need no man and I never would need one. I wasn't about to put myself through that and end up hurt and angry. That will never be me. I'll die alone and with no kids, it is what it is.*

I closed my eyes, and allowed the flavor from the Patron to soak my body with the bliss of the night.

The sirens echoed through the neighborhood, filling my ears with peace, reminding me that the streets never slept, and that the ones who stayed awake had a shot to live forever.

I relaxed my body and allowed sleep to locate me.

Jiip

"Shit that jewelry hard as fuck!" I said while looking through Reecy Pooh's bag of goodies.

"I know it's nice nigga. That's why I need my money. I don't work for free." She said while laying back in the bed against the pillow.

I looked at her sexy, thick, chocolate ass body and my manhood pulsated at the thought of what I was about to do to her ass. She reminded me of a dark-skinned Trina, and she was definitely one of the baddest bitches I had ever had the luxury of fucking with. Why she ended up fucking with a nigga like me I had no clue. Some bitches always searching for 2% of what they're missing in a nigga who don't have 98% of what they need. Wasn't my concern though.

"You be so wired up bitch you need to relax man." I said while thinking about how I was going to fuck her from the back and nut in that pussy.

"Quit calling me out my damn name nigga. Fuck you mean. You's a bitch."

I laughed, unconcerned with words at this point.

"O.K. Shiddd, you say you wanted $40,000 for all of it right?" I said while licking my lips.

"Yea. I'ma give you $120,000 worth of shit for $40k."

"Shit aight bet. I'ma give you $20k right now, and I'll give you the other 20K when I bust the safe open tomorrow evening. Do we got a deal?"

"A safe? Nigga you don't even know what's in a got damn safe to be promising me 20 more thousand. You sound crazy as hell right now. And what safe anyway nigga?" Reecy Pooh asked, her voice ghetto as fuck and irritating at times.

I grabbed my phone and pulled up my Instagram account. I scrolled down the timeline and stopped on a post that had just been posted about 5 minutes ago. I pressed play.

"These fuck niggaz killed my fuckin mama! I swear fo' God... When I find out who did this shit, yo whole family gone feel my fuckin wrath!" The man in the video yelled through angry tears. It was an emotional video, and he flipped the camera around to show police officers casing the scene.

I put my phone away and looked in her eyes. She was obviously shaken up, but I also think that was what my appeal was to her. I represented something that was completely foreign to her life. Something that you couldn't just find on a daily basis... A real stone cold thugged-out ass killer. I know that shit turned her on.

"Shid shawty, if you don't think it's $20K in a safe I got from Block Sushi, then I'll just get the one situation and just give you the $20k. I'll let you sell the other stuff to somebody else."

I knew the wheels were turning in her head. I knew how hard it was to sell shit in the streets, hell that's why I never bothered, and took shit instead. I didn't have the patience or the skills it took to be a salesperson. I'ma take-person.

"Aight nah... I'll fuck with you on the $40k." Reecy Pooh said as she smiled at me. "Where the money at?" She asked, still thinking about business.

"Hold on, lemme go get it."

I walked out of the room and shut the door. I walked down the hallway and grabbed the $20K out of the cereal box. Then I walked down to the room Albert stayed in whenever he stayed over. Albert was dark and skinny, like the complexion of Kevin Durant, except he was much much shorter and even skinnier than the NBA star.

"Al." I said as I knocked on the door. "Aye Al."

"Sup Unc?" He said from behind the door.

"Yeen jackin off in there is ya?" I didn't wanna walk in on that shit no more. Hell fuck nawl.

"Nah Unc. What's up?" He said, and opened the door. "What's up?"

"Shidddd," I said slowly. "Slide ya Unc some of them Bill Cosbies fa' dis bitch."

"Say no mo." Al said as he pulled an Excedrin pill bottle out of his pocket.

He handed me a single pill.

"Damn all I get is one?" I asked.

"Unc, cut that one pill into 4 sections. You only need one section."

I walked out of the room and back into the kitchen. I mixed up some Hennessy and cranberry for both of us and I dropped the whole pill into her drink. I didn't have time to be cutting up no pill. It wasn't like she was gon drink the whole cup of Henny anyways. Shiddd.

I stirred the cup and watched as the pill dissolved, and then went back into the room. I handed her the cup and sat back and relaxed. I could tell she was already horny and ready to fuck, but I didn't want shit that easy. I never wanted shit that was easy. I wanted to do mine a different way, it was just a sick fetish of mine.

"What you done put in my cup nigga?" She laughed as she looked at me.

I frowned at her trying to figure out how the fuck she knew I put anything in there.

She smiled and shook her head. "I'm just joking nigga damn ol' crazy ass nigga. Have a got damn sense of humor."

"Nah you shut the hell up and have a got damn drink." For some reason her saying that made my heart beat faster. Like how the fuck you know what I did bitch. It bothered me for real and I didn't know why, but eventually I got over her comment. I couldn't really be that got damn mad because I put something in that shit for real.

After a couple of minutes, her eyes were glazed over. "Damn this Henny gwood ah fuqqqqq." She slurred.

"Damnnnnn." She said and started smacking her mouth loud. She opened her mouth and rubbed her tongue slowly against her teeth like she had just discovered something nasty in her mouth. Then she took her finger and rubbed her top gum. "My gum wah' itchin."

She twisted her lips and closed her eyes. I caught the cup before she spilled it on the bed and sat if on the counter.

"You ok baby?" I asked her, to which she didn't reply.

She leaned back against the pillow, spaced out, exactly where I wanted her.

I unzipped my pants.

MS. LATTIS

"You sure we can get away with this Otis?" I asked while looking into my fiance's eyes. I loved this man just as much as he loved me, and nothing would ever change that as long as I lived.

"Definitely Henrietta. I don't see a way we can get caught as long as we're in and out the way we say we're gon' be. This is Atlanta, so as soon as we get the money, we gon get lost in traffic." Otis said as we arrived to our destination.

It was the Sun Trust bank on Luckie Street, and the plan was for us to hit the bank and ride into the sunset.

"Do you want me to just drive while you handle it? I don't wanna be in your way... I can be the getaway driver if you need me to be." I said nervously.

"Nah you're going in with me on this one. You'll be fine baby."

We pulled up and parked. He handed me a gun and hopped out with his concealed. I watched as he walked around the car and tapped on my door. I got out with my gun in my purse, and we walked into the bank like a couple.

He wasted no time. "Everybody's hands UP! Hands in the fuckin AIR! Everybody! Don't let me catch you tryna' play me!" He screamed while running around the room like a mad man.

I stopped hesitating and ran to the counter with my gun out while he ran around the room making everyone was on the ground. I was filling up a medium sized trash bag that I'd stuffed in my purse for that very reason. My adrenaline was rushing as I went from counter to counter filling that bag up with cash.

When it was done I couldn't believe how heavy it was. "Baby we did it!" He saw that I was done and instantly started running for the door. I started running too, and then the moment that altered my entire life happened... I tripped up over my own foot, and hit the ground. I dropped the bag and money spilled everywhere.

"Oh no!" I screamed. He turned and saw what had happened and jumped down to help me put some of the money back in the bag.

"Shit we gotta leave the rest, let's go!" He screamed.

I stood up, and then his eyes got wide and he pushed me back to the floor.

Pow! Pow!

A civilian with a firearm tried to kill me— Otis shielded me and took the shots for me. Otis' blood spilled on my shirt and panic seized my body like never before.

"Run Henrietta." Otis screamed as he grabbed his gun and turned back around having a shootout with the gun holder.

I took what money I had and ran out of the doors of the bank and into the getaway car. I sat there waiting on Otis to run out of the bank and get in the car. I heard one more gunshot, and then silence. I hesitated to drive... Refusing to believe that my fiancé wasn't going to come running out of that bank. I heard sirens in the distance, but nothing else mattered except the fact that the love of my life wasn't coming back to my car.

I drove slowly at first, my eyes still on the rear-view mirror. It was all my fault that Otis wasn't coming back, and I really wanted to turn myself in because life no longer mattered to me. Otis was my happiness, my life, my everything, and with my luck, I'd managed to ruin my life in one trip.

***

I woke up drenched in sweat. Over the years I'd had that nightmare a few times, and it always gave me the urge to wanna get high once the dream was over. I hadn't had that dream since I cleaned my life up, but with Ice wanting to talk about robberies so much, it stirred up some memories that I'd prefer to leave in the past.

I was fiendin' for a rock.

I needed a hit bad as hell. The last class I went through told me whenever I felt like I was about to relapse, to call them or call a family member. I dialed Ice's number, but it just rang.

I began to panic more and more. I called my instructor from the recovery clinic, but his phone just rang also.

I started to shake, and sweat beads became a fashion statement on my forehead. I knew what I needed to do, verses what I wanted to do... Class taught me to understand my needs in order to understand how powerful the needs were verses my wants. I went in the kitchen and poured a cup of sweet tea. I needed to dissolve my wants... I needed to swallow my pride. I couldn't risk relapsing at that age. Ice would have a heart attack if anything happened to me. Finally, I felt my body relaxing, and reality coming back into the picture.

I grabbed a scented Glade candle off of the counter top, and took it to the kitchen table. Using a long-nose automatic lighter, I pressed the button and watched the flame hug the wick. The sound of the fire sizzling against the white wick sent a chill through my body. It was like staring at the flame against a rock... The heat sucking the juices and natural beauty and strengths out of the crack cocaine. The aroma running away from the fire and through my body in a hectic pursuit to find peace.

My cell phone rang, and when I saw the caller ID, I was finally able to snap out of the zone I was sinking into.

"Good morning Ice." I tried to say it calmly, trying not to let her hear the trembling that was in my voice. It didn't work.

"What's wrong with you?"

I didn't say anything right away, but I knew that I would have to answer her question. She deserved that much.

PATRON

It was 3 AM when I got up that morning. I'd given away the money I needed in order to pay my rent with, but luckily I had worked something out with an associate to do a job with him early that morning. The catch was, he didn't tell me what the job was going to be. He only told me to be ready to go early so that he could drop me back off so that I could also keep the schedule I had with my landscape clientele.

I was up at 3, and the horn to a truck blew at around 3:07. He wasn't playing no games about being ready. I didn't even have time to eat breakfast that morning. I put my black boots on, grabbed a bottled water and left out the door. By the time I stepped out he was blowing the horn again, so I didn't even get a chance to lock the door to my house. I felt like I was causing him to be late when I was the one who needed the favor, so I tried to hurry up and move faster.

I walked to the passenger side door, but the interior cab was full. I hopped on the back of the truck with 2 other men. It was warm outside so I was wearing a black t-shirt, but these guys had on sweaters. I knew the wind was chillier in the morning, and that they had to experience a slight wind chill since they were on the back of the truck, but those sweaters were entirely too hot and unreasonable.

We finally arrived to our destination, which looked like some sort of farm. My associate Warrin, hopped out of the truck and handed me two set of gloves and a bottle of rubbing alcohol.

"What I'ma do with this?" I asked him with a confused look on my face.

"Oh you'll see Patrick. Come with us."

There was a lot of noise being made inside of the large building we were walking toward, and I had no clue what it was until Warrin opened the door. When we got in, it sounded like there were a million chickens inside the place.

"Today I just need you to go down these rows and grab the eggs out. Do not crack the eggs, do not drop the eggs. Eggs is money!" Warrin said as he handed me a large stack of egg cartons.

"Carry one egg carton at a time. If you ear the hen cackling, let the hen finish. Do not interrupt the hen. If you accidentally break an egg in the nest, clean it up immediately! If the hen discovers that the egg is edible, then the hen will be eating the eggs the next time they lay. Don't ruin my chickens Patrick."

"Got it." I said, catching on as quickly as he was speaking. My only mission was to pay my house note so I could continue to support Ice. Nothing else mattered... I didn't care what I had to do to make sure that she was ok in this cold world. One day I would have her... One day she would be my wife, I'd dreamed about this, and I knew it was going to happen one day.

I walked up to the first nest and they were jumping up and down before I even got there. They weren't cackling, it seemed they were going crazy for some reason. I saw the eggs in plain view, so there was no point in not getting them.

Bawwwk! Bawwwwwwwk! Bawwwk! Bawwwk! Bawwwwk!

That scared the shit out of me. Those damn birds were flapping and jumping up and down as if I was coming to kill them. Man all I wanted was the fuckin eggs. "Shut up you fuckin birds!" I yelled as I kept trying to reach in there to get the eggs I saw.

There were 4 perfect white eggs, and I needed to retrieve them peacefully. I pushed my arm into the cage a little further, and I suddenly felt something snap around my gloved finger.

"What the fuck!" I yelled. I looked into the cage and saw a snake.

"Yo! Man it's a fuckin snake in here!" I yelled out so Warrin could hear me.

He came running. "Hurry and get the chickens out!" He yelled.

"What? Man you crazy as hell! I'm not reaching in there and getting shit!"

"Patrick get the chickens before the snake kills them!"

That was my final straw. I couldn't do this shit. That nigga was really trippin. He talking about a fucking group of chickens about to lose their life when I'm a whole human-being, being asked to save they ass from a fuckin snake.

"How the hell I'm supposed to save the chickens from the snake man?"

"Reach in there and grab them!" He screamed at me angrily.

I shook my head and laughed. That nigga had to have either lost my mind or really felt some type of way about my life. I pulled my gloves off and walked outside of the chicken farm. The reason I had my own landscaping company was because I liked being my own boss. I couldn't stand for others to talk to me like I'm crazy or incompetent, and I definitely never asked anybody who ever worked for me to do anything life threatening. Whenever I saw a snake while cleaning a yard, we killed it if we could, and got the hell on out the way.

I sat on a wooden bench and checked the time. I had plenty of time to get home, change into my work clothes, pick Jose up and get started on our first yard of the day.

"Hey Patrick." Warrin said, sticking his head out of the door. "My fault about that situation bro. It's just customary to save the chickens... Snakes are a common thing with sneaking in chicken farms. We save the chickens, and get rid of the snakes."

"Hey man, I'm not knocking it. Do ya' thing, it's just not for me. Thanks for the opportunity, but I'ma have to get back home."

Warrin was insulted. "You don't wanna give it another try? I mean, you're already out here..."

"Nah, I'm good my guy."

Why the hell was this man tryna pressure me to help him with those fuckin eggs?

"Aight bet. Well then... You can wait in the office in the chair while we finish up. I'm guessing you need a ride home right?"

"Yea I do."

"O.K. cool, yea I'll unlock the office and you can rest until we're done."

I was a bit drowsy from waking up so early, so that sounded like a perfect scenario for me. I had a couple hours before I needed to get back to the house anyways. I'd use those couple hours to sleep before picking up Jose. I turned my phone off to save my battery.

JOSE

Patron being this late had me nervously pacing back and forth in my living room. I'd called his phone several times and it continued to go to voice mail. Our first job was supposed to be at 7 this morning, and here it was 9:30 AM. The reason I stayed around was because I didn't want to miss him in case he did show up late, but it was becoming very clear that something was wrong.

I had a car, but I hardly ever drove it, however, Patron had been a friend to me when nobody else in the United States was. I made my way to the states in the back of a trailer of an 18 wheeler with about 119 other Mexicans. Temperatures in the back of the trailer reached well over 100 degrees, and there was limited ventilation, so we all had to take turns breathing through holes that were placed throughout the length of the trailer.

37 Mexicans didn't make it to their destinations alive, but we knew what we were facing before we signed up and paid the $2,000 transport fee. The driver agreed to risk major prison time for that amount, but looking back at it, if I was him I would have done the same exact thing. When I got to Houston, I was able to get a fake driver's license through some Mexicans who were already established, but I was told to be extra careful with the license because the information belonged to a real person.

After I got my license, I had major problems getting a job in Houston, and was living homeless for months before another Mexican told me that one of the people who came with us on the back of the truck ended up getting a job in Atlanta GA. That's all I needed to hear. I jumped on the Greyhound bus and headed to Atlanta, where I ran into Patrick, or like I call him; Patron.

I'd saw him at a gas station and asked him if he knew of anyone who was hiring. He told me to hop in the truck, and I made my first $100 in America on that day. My life, and the life of my family back home in Mexico had been much better since meeting Patron. My wife didn't have to worry, my kids were good, and I even had money left over after taking care of my family in Mexico. The plan was to get established and move my family over to Atlanta, GA, but when Donald Trump became president, things started taking a turn for the worse.

Many of the people who came with me on that truck shipment all those years back, had been rounded up and deported, and forced to start back over from the bottom. When I realized this, I started sending more and more money over to my wife and told her to make some investments in case I ended up in that situation. Every day I was living life looking over my shoulder. I was an honest person, all I wanted to do was work and provide a decent living for my family ya know? I didn't understand what the harm was all about. I wasn't taking any jobs away from any Americans, because nobody wanted to work with Patron but me.

I helped him build his landscaping brand from the ground up, and many times I felt so honored to be given a chance by him, I'd do the work myself and let him relax. He deserved it, and I was going to be forever loyal to him, win, lose, or draw. There was no scenario greater than loyalty, and I told him that every time we talked about life. Coming from Mexico, loyalty was just as important as breathing. We were a proud group of people, and we lived or died by our word.

***

When I arrived at Patron's house, it was 10:30 AM, and his work truck was still in the yard. His place was only so big, so I had to park my car in the road beside his mailbox. I walked up to the door and knocked on it as hard as I could. I knocked for a few minutes and figured he had to have overslept, so I knocked harder and yelled his name out.

"Patron! Open up!" I beat my fist against the door even harder, but he didn't answer. I was about to just break into his house and find out what was going on with him, but when I looked back, I saw a cop car drive up the street. That was the last thing I needed in my life at the moment, so I turned and started walking towards the car. I would have to just wait until Patron woke up.

I opened the car door and just as I was getting inside, I saw flashing lights pull behind my vehicle. It was my first ever encounter with police, and my heart was beating straight out of my chest. Just that quickly I realized how hot the Atlanta sun was, and the heat of the situation felt 10 times stronger than the heat in the back of the 18 wheeler coming to America.

"License and insurance sir." The officer said, while sitting his hand on his weapon.

I knew enough not to argue with the man, so I grabbed my license and handed him my insurance for the car.

"What are you doing over here in this area? You got relatives here or something?" The cop asked.

"I came to see my bossman."

"Bossman huh? Where does your bossman live?" The cop was looking at me with a deranged look on his face.

"That house right there sir." I said, pointing to Patron's house. I had no idea what the problem was with this guy. I had done nothing wrong.

"Oh really?" He asked while rubbing his chin. "And what's up with all of those Western Union forms in the back seat of your car?"

I felt my heart sink to the ground. Why didn't I think to hide them? Why did I still have them? This wasn't going to go too well.

"I sent money to Mexico to my family."

"To Mexico? You're not a U.S. citizen?" He asked.

"I am sir."

"Do you mind if I see one of your Western Union forms?" The cop asked, digging deeper in suspicion.

I didn't know what to say to the officer. It seemed I was stuck between a rock and a hard place. The name on the Western Union receipt was my real name, and the name on the driver's license was a whole different person. I remained silent and sat there, wishing he would just disappear and leave me alone. There was nothing else to discuss at this point, so I just had to let whatever was going to happen, happen.

"Is there a problem officer?" I heard a familiar voice ask the cop.

"Step away from the vehicle! Get back! Put your hands up now!" The cop screamed as he grabbed his weapon.

"What the fuck?" Patron spoke, confused. "What did I do? I just got back from a chicken farm. What—"

"Hands up!" The cop screamed as he drew his weapon and pointed it at Patron.

I was getting mad as fuck because Patron didn't do shit to deserve that. "What the fuck you pointing the gun at him for?" I yelled.

"Shut up! Both of you think you're slick! Running a drug operation! Funneling money and drugs from Mexico! Put your hands up now! Both of you! Now! Keep them up!"

The officer was delirious. He pressed a button on his radio and requested back-up. "Send some Immigration and Customs Enforcement officers out here as well. I think I have a situation."

"Hands where I can see them! Do you have any weapons on your possession?" He asked Patron aggressively.

"No sir, I don't!" Patron yelled back.

"This guy works for you he tells me!"

"He does!"

"Then that's all the reason I'll need to search your property!" The officer yelled. He grabbed his radio again and requested a warrant for searching Patron's house.

I closed my eyes, not believing what was happening to us. It wasn't like he was going to find any drugs in my car or in Patron's house, so he was really wasting his time. I hated the fact that he'd called Ice agents however, but I felt I could still get around them being that I had a legit driver's license, and hadn't broken any laws. I started to relax a little, feeling more confident about our situation.

Two back up officers arrived, and one put handcuffs on Patron first, and sat him on the ground in front of my vehicle. Then they pulled me out the car and handcuffed my hands behind my back. They sat me down right beside Patron while holding their weapons drawn at us.

"Officer calm down... We're handcuffed, so it's no reason to keep your guns pointed at us." Patron spoke up.

"Shut up you fuckin nigger. You and your fuckin Mexican spic of a friend think you're slick. Trying to sell drugs in our country, you're the fucking scums of the earth, both of you! I could put a bullet in both of your heads right now, report it as a drug bust and nobody would give a fuck!"

Patron got quiet, and I definitely didn't have anything to say.

I heard the other officers as they pulled up and jumped out of their cars. One of them walked up to the officer holding the weapon. "Officer we have a search warrant as requested, we're about to conduct a search based on your suspicions."

"I'm sure you're going to be pleased with my suspicions." The officer said as he stared into the other police officer's eyes.

"Yes sir. We're about to check the residence now."

At least an hour had gone by while sitting on that ground wearing those uncomfortable handcuffs. One of the officers walked over to the officer who had been responsible for all of this madness. "Sir, the FBI want to take over. They said this is their case."

"What?" The officer yelled. "This is my case! It doesn't belong to the FBI! Absolutely not!"

Me and Patron looked at each other at the same time. I frowned because I knew that my time in America was up. I shook my head and prepared to continue on my journey. I could tell Patron's feelings were hurt, but in life sometimes we just have to do what we have to do.

"My apologies my amigo." I said to him, meaning every word. "We'll see each other again. It's going to be ok."

Patron sighed. I hated the fact that I was letting him down, but all I could do at that point was see what the outcome was going to be.

Two men wearing navy blue suits and ties walked up to the officers just as they were arguing. "I'm Agent Braxnell, FBI, and this is Agent Sluke. We'll take it from here officers, thank you." They flashed their badges at the officers and it appeared that those badges took all of the steam out of them.

The officer handed him the key to the handcuffs and his business card. The agents took the items watched as the officers walked back to their cars without further complaint. The officers turned their lights off and drove off, leaving us with the two agents.

"Patrick. Patron. Which do you prefer I call you?" Agent Braxnell asked.

"Patrick."

"O.K. Patrick, you'll come with me. You take Emmanuel." He said and smirked.
When he said my real name, I felt the same way the officers felt. All of my energy left my body and I knew this was it.

Agent Sluke picked me up off of the ground and took me to his vehicle. He turned the air conditioning on and leaned back in his seat. "Emmanuel you know what I want from you in order to stay in exchange for your stay in America. Otherwise you'll be deported to the hell-hole you escaped from, you know I know all of your skeletons." He smiled at me deviously.

"I don't have nothing to be afraid of agent. And also, I don't have anything to tell you."

"Oh but you do have plenty to tell me. You see... We were watching you the moment you arrived in Atlanta. We caught the guy who told you about Atlanta, and he told me where everyone else was. We started following you, and then we ended up learning about Patron's little operation."

"What? Patron is innocent completely. He gave me a job. A legitimate job."

"Yea, but what about him masterminding this multi-million-dollar theft ring?"

"What theft ring?" I asked incredulously.

"Oh stop it. We've watched him send his girl out on these jobs, stealing all of these items. We've watched it all and documented it. Now we could be wrong of course... but it would be on you to correct it... but you'd have to correct it by telling me other information first."

I sighed. "What information man?"

He tossed a picture of my old friend, Dominguez into my lap. "Your friend is in Houston living like a kingpin. Help us get to him. We know the history with you two. He feels like he owes you, and you don't want anything to do with the lifestyle. So help us... then we'll help you, and we'll also help Patron."

"Fuck you." I spat and sat back in my seat. I would never go out like that. It was that moment I knew I was going to have to figure something out to make up for the trouble Patron was about to go through. I hated they were fucking with him because of me, but if it was the last thing I did before I did, I was going to make sure to make up for my flaws.

PATRON

I sat on the steps of my house in silence while waiting on the agent to say a word to me. In the beginning all he did was stare at me like I was crazy, or like he was trying to figure out what he was going to say to me. It didn't matter to me one way or the other though, because I knew I had done nothing wrong. I was a working man in America, a black business owner who took pride in waking up and going to work every day. One who took pride in handling his business, and being different from what the statistics reflected regarding the black male race.

The agent's phone rang, and he answered it. "O.k. Alright. All right then, let me handle that real quick. You sure? Okie dokie."

"Aight listen." The agent said as he stared me in the eyes. "Your little friend just told us everything."

"Huh?" I frowned up at him. I had no idea what the fuck was he even talking about. "Told y'all everything about what?"

"About your stolen goods. About the operation you were running with your girlfriend. About you receiving stolen goods. See we've been watching for quite a while since you and your girlfriend have been stealing at least $100,000 worth of items per month. That's too much damn money."

I felt instantly betrayed, and knew I had to call my mother as soon as possible. I had no idea why Jose would tell them a lie on me, but I guess he had to do it in order to stay in America. Then I thought about what would possibly happen if they sent him back to Mexico. I didn't want him to die over there. My demeanor changed. Fuck it, I thought. I'll just deal with whatever the consequences are.

"O.K. what about it?" I asked him.

The agent was surprised at my statement.

"What about what?" He asked.

"What about my operation? What do you want from me?"

He frowned up and walked closer to me. "Are you going to just sit here and say it's true? This is actually your operation or were you buying these stolen goods from somebody?" He asked while he was standing directly in front of me.

"It's my operation. I don't buy shit, I sell it, or I keep it moving."

The agent shook his head and grabbed my shirt. "You think this is a fuckin game don't you? You know who we're really after, so let's stop this cat and mouse game. These bitches are out here stealing Rolexes and living like Queens, so stop defending and playing and tell us more about them. We'll let you and your little boyfriend go, but give us what we need."

So this is what it was all about. I thought as I smirked. I hated I was about to be the cause of Jose going back to Mexico, but I promised myself that I would make up for it some type of way. I was never giving him any information on Ice. That was off-limits period.

"Help us Patron. You helping us, will get you out of trouble, and it'll even help Emmanuel— sorry, you know him as Jose. It'll even help Jose stay in America." He said to me like it was a beautiful deal.

"Fuck you." I spat. "Gone ahead and lock me up."

"You going to jail for a bitch who don't care nothing about you? You gon' take this dumb ass charge? Because if you really want this theft ring charge, I'm going to fuckin give it to you."

"Run that shit." I said, but honestly I had no idea the depths and the seriousness of what I was getting into.

ICE

Tears soaked my face as I sat there listening to Ms. Lattis' story. The entire time I'd known her, I'd never known that fact about her. I never knew she lost someone she loved while on a job. I never understood the reasoning behind her wanting me to stick with the stores until that morning. It hurt me to hear her in so much pain from a memory.

"Ms. Lattis do you need me to come over?" I asked, checking the time. It was early for me.

"No sugar, I just needed to vent. I guess I've been through so much in life that it overwhelms me sometimes. I went from being engaged to being in the streets, to being in the crack houses–"

I interrupted her. "To recovery Ms. Lattis. You went from all of those situations to being a better person, and being in remission of your cancer, and I'm proud of you! Have I told you that you make me proud and happy? You do!"

Ms. Lattis was crying while listening to me talk. "Sugar, I get so tired of feeling so helpless. I feel like I'm no good to you. My body is no good anymore. I feel like–"

"I need you to stop thinking like that. Stop feeling like that. You mean the world to me Ms. Lattis. You don't realize the influence you have over my life. I owe you my life because you gave me so much of yours."

"Baby you don't owe me a thing!" Ms. Lattis said to me. "I want you to live your life for you, stop living so much for me. I want you to have a family. To find you a man you're compatible with, one who loves and respects you as a woman. Bring me a grandbaby."

That blew my mind completely. As many times as I'd referred to her as my mother, she always rejected that title. Yet, today she fully stepped into that title. "Alright... Sounds fair. But I don't know where to start with bringing you a grandbaby."

We both started laughing.

"You gotta start with finding you a man that's decent." She said, laughing.

"Lawddddd, I don't know how this is going to work."

"Ice don't act like you're not an attractive girl. Everytime we go somewhere; you have all these men staring at you. Sometimes you have to stare back! You don't have not one person who shows you some type of real interest? Girl have you ever even had sex?"

I was so over this conversation. "Alright Ms. Lattis. This conversation is over."

"Call me Mom, and this conversation is just beginning." She said while giving a small chuckle.

"Well Mom..." I hesitated to let the words linger for a little while. "I love you."

"I love you too sugar, but I need you to bring me a grandbaby."

"Okkkk and I'll talk with you later, this is awkwardddd."

"You need to let a man knock the cobwebs off that thang."

"Oh my God. Bye." I hurried to hang the phone up. That was the most uncomfortable I'd ever been while talking to Ms. Lattis. I shook my head and laid back in my bed.

I grabbed the remote and turned the television on to see if me and Reecy Pooh had made the news for our work from the previous day. The first story was about some old lady who'd gotten shot while sleeping. The second story was about some guys who robbed a Taco Bell. The third story was about a group of people who robbed the Bentley dealership. There was no story about me and Reecy Pooh.

I took a deep breath and closed my eyes. We just weren't doing it big enough to get recognition. Every time I told her that we weren't getting recognition, she would say that it's a good thing. However, who the hell wanted to be the best at something and never get any credit for it? I'd listened to Ms. Lattis tell me about her losing her fiancé, and honestly, it only made me want to rob a bank that much more.

I wanted the opportunity to have a powerful story like that. I'd never been in love before so I wouldn't be able to understand her pain completely. All I understood was that I really wanted to rob a bank. I was going to have to make it happen one way or the other. With Reecy Pooh or without her. It had grown into a deep desire, and something I'd began thinking of every day, even while boosting, in my heart I wanted to be robbing.

RHONDO

Reecy Pooh never came home that night. I'd been up the majority of the night waiting, but she never walked back in the house. I'd started regaining some of my basic motor skills– not that they'd ever left me completely, but it was the fact that I had to retrain some of them to instill muscle memory. I popped another

Percocet, thought about what I needed to do in order to get back right.

I was really tired of the wheelchair shit, and I was going to make it a point to start walking around, I was going to regain my strength. I was going to clean and shower myself, not matter how difficult it was going to be. I knew that I would eventually get it right. I *had* to get it right so I could go get my revenge in the streets.

The phone conversation I had with Stats really boosted my determination and motivation. He told me that niggas' in the streets were actually laughing at me for being shot. He told me he had to put the pistol on one nigga for joking about the shit, but he told me that it was too many people talking crazy out there. Talking about how I got caught slippin' like a lame, how I'm some type of easy target.

I couldn't wait to hit those streets and show them that I'm far from an easy target. The streets were going to turn red as soon as I could get my body together. All of those jokes and comments from the streets had made me angry, but none of those comments had me as angry as the rumor about my girlfriend fuckin' with Jiip.

I'd heard the rumor before getting shot, but I didn't believe it. I'd known Jiip a long time, but only knew him just to be a robbing ass nigga, never no type of playa ass nigga. He didn't give a fuck about a bitch long enough to fuck another nigga's. So my guess was that either my bitch was pressed, or she saw something in him that she didn't see in me. Shit was crazy, but that was the street life. You gon fuck other niggas hoes, so you can't expect other niggas not to fuck yo hoes.

One thing about it though, as soon as I heard the rumor, I called my side bitch Rosina and told her to come pick me up ASAP. She said she was at her baby daddy's spot at the moment, but that she would be over to pick me up bright and early if my chick hadn't made it home yet. Shit my bitch wasn't nowhere in sight. I sent Rosina a text, letting her know to scoop me up in her Trail Blazer. I was going to rehabilitate myself at her crib. Rosina was mixed with Spanish and white, so she really knew how to treat a nigga for real. She never argued with me, and always made me feel like the king that I knew I was.

The vibes that she gave off were going to be perfect for me. I couldn't feel like less of a man with a woman who made me feel like I was the only man in the world. The only reason I didn't make her my main chick was because I didn't like her feet.

I know it sounds crazy, but that bitch had some ugly ass toes bruh. Body was banging, face like a super model, titties done by a professional, ass like two volleyballs, skin perfect, smile gorgeous... Rosina was sexy as fuck! But her toes looked like 10 gremlins all angry at each other. Man come to think of it, I don't even know if she had all ten toes bruh. Her shit was fucked up.

Reecy Pooh hadn't called, hadn't text me, hadn't checked on me at all. The way I saw it, she basically only did the bare minimum, and then she left me for dead. That was all the extra motivation I needed. Funny how your girl can try to motivate you in a positive way and it does nothing to help, but the minute she crossed you, you found all the motivation you never knew you even possessed. Black men operated like that, simply because deep down inside we were all waiting to be crossed by the person claiming they love us.

Ain't no muthafuckin love in 2017. I knew better.

REECY POOH

I woke up in so much main that I thought I was on my death bed. My neck hurt, my back hurt, my wrist had a bruise on it, and my face felt funny. I looked down and seen that all of my clothes were gone and that I was in a foreign place. I looked around the room trying to remember the events from the night before. Everything was fuzzy for a second, then overwhelming pressure increased from the pit of my soul.

"Jiip!" I screamed out.

Nobody responded. I quickly reached for my backpack containing my Rolexes, bracelets, rings, and chains, and the entire backpack was gone. "Fuck!" I screamed.

I jumped up from the bed and a creamy liquid shot out of my vagina. "Oh my God!" I screamed. "What the fuck!"

I ran to the bathroom and threw up in the sink. "What the fuck!" I was hyperventilating, gasping for oxygen and understanding.

I looked in the mirror and half of my face was swollen. It looked like Jiip used me for a fucking punching bag! I was going to kill that nigga if it was the last thing I did.

I turned the shower on immediately. I felt sick as fuck, and didn't even realize the tears running down my face until a tear dropped into the cut and burned me. "Oh my God!"

I didn't know who to call or who I could turn to at that point. If I called Ice, she would judge me because she told me she didn't like the fact that I was cheating on Rhondo in the first place. I'd told her about how he cheated on me so many times, but she couldn't possibly understand because she'd never been in a relationship before anyways. She wasn't going to be able to help me in this scenario.

I had two other girlfriends I could call, but it would be too embarrassing because they were all with me motivating me to leave Rhondo for Jiip based on the way I said he treated me. I didn't want to tell them what happened because then it was going to seem like I couldn't keep a fuckin man. I was so hurt and felt so betrayed that all I could think about was the ultimate revenge. I hated the fact that he'd taken advantage of me. I hated it!

I heard my phone ring in the other room, and I walked out to see who it was. I glanced at the caller ID and saw Rhondo's name on it. I definitely couldn't talk to him at that point after walking out on him last night. Hindsight is always perfect vision, and in hindsight, I realized that all I should have done that night was kicking it with my man, no matter how many problems we'd been having. Rhondo would have never hurt me that bad no matter how bad of a person he was at times. It took a dirty dog devil to stoop this low to hurt me.

After Rhondo's call ended, my phone rang again, this time Jiip's name was on the screen.

"What the fuck you want nigga?" I screamed into the phone, angry as fuck.

"Thank God you're ok baby!" He yelled into the phone, out of breath. "Thank God!"

"What? Nigga you did this to me! You did this to me! You bitch ass nigga! I hate you nigga! I'ma kill you nigga! I'ma kill you!" I was boiling hot on the inside, and I didn't wanna talk to this nigga on the phone, I wanted his ass dead! I hung the phone up, and the phone rang again, this time it was a Facetime.

"What nigga?" I screamed at Jiip through tears. "What the fuck you want nigga? What???"

Jiip flipped the camera around, and I saw that he was in some dark warehouse.

"What the fuck nigga! Where is my jewelry! I'ma kill—" My voice got stuck in my throat when I seen Albert's dead body. *What the fuck?*

"They robbed us last night baby! Them niggaz came in with AKs, a baseball bat, rope, and duct tape. They hit me with a baseball bat, and the next thing I know, I woke up in this warehouse. Thank God you're ok!" Jiip screamed at me.

I didn't know what to believe anymore, I was so confused. Tears ran down my face at a rapid pace. "Who raped me Jiip?" I screamed into the phone.

"Say what? Somebody raped you? I'ma KILL them niggaz! Straight the fuck up! I'ma kill them niggaz I swear to God! Baby get dressed, and get the fuck out that house asap. Get the fuck out of there! I'll meet you at the Comfort Inn in the next 30 minutes."

He hung up the phone and I sat there, stunned. I didn't know what the fuck happened, but there was no way he was lying to me with his best friend and protégé laying on the ground dead as fuck. He had no reason to kill Albert, because Albert really looked up to him. He definitely didn't have a reason to rape me because I was willing to give it up to him, so his words were starting to make more sense. He also didn't have a reason to steal from me because he knew I would give him whatever the hell he asked for honestly.

I went and jumped in the shower, eager to get to the bottom of that shit. Somebody was gon' face the wrath of a black woman scorned, and didn't even know it yet. Somebody was gon' die.

Jiip

I hung the phone up and shook my head at how naïve Reecy Pooh was. I knew I had some serious problems going on with me mentally, but I told her that shit up front when I first met her. She laughed it off back then, as if I was joking. I was far from joking... I just knew I liked to do shit that other people may not find as appealing as me. I didn't like to be given a got-damn thing, I was going to die as a taker. Period.

"Albert get up lil homey. She went for the shit."

Albert got up off of the ground and wiped some dirt and makeup off of his face.

"Nah Al, you gon' have to shower and clean that shit off. All that movie blood, all that shit gotta' be washed off with soap."

Al nodded his head in agreement. He really loved Jiip's style, and knew that one day he was going to be just like him. He didn't have a father figure in his life, so whatever he saw Jiip engage in became law to him. He met him when he was 15 years old, and had helped him on many an occasion, all to Jiip's satisfaction.

"Is it a shower in here?" Al asked while wiping some of the fake blood off of his face.

"Yea it's one in the office. Check this out... I'ma give you $10,000 cash for helping me out with this shit. Is that cool? What chu think?"

Albert had a huge smile on his face. "Hell yea $10,000 is perfect!" He started thinking about how many pairs of Jordans he was going to buy with the hefty sum of money.

"Aight bet. Shit, I'ma give you $2,000 right now and the rest later."

Albert didn't even think twice. "Aight Unc. Preciate it. Hell yea!"

ICE

I was knocked out snoring when I heard someone's fist banging against my front door. I grabbed my pistol thinking it was the police, and I knew what my philosophy was regarding going to prison. I just wasn't going to do it period. I slipped my shorts on, a pair of sneakers and a tank top and peeped out the window to see how many officers were out there.

I immediately calmed down when I saw the familiar vehicle in the parking spot beside my Honda. I walk out of my room, down the hall, and opened the door.

"I'm so sorry Ice!" Reecy Pooh cried as she fell into my arms. Her face was swollen and she had cuts on her arm and neck. I was so confused and lost, but I could feel the negative energy that was eating away at her.

"Come in so I can close the door Reecy." I said as I looked behind her making sure nobody was following her.

I locked the door and hugged Reecy Pooh, not knowing what was going on with her, and not knowing how I could fix the situation. I knew it had to be serious though, because Reecy never came to my place, and on top of that, she hardly ever got out the house before noon.

"I fucked up Ice! I really fucked up! I'm so sorry! I'm sorry!"

"Why do you keep apologizing to me?" I asked her. "You've done me no wrong."

"I got robbed!" Reecy Pooh screamed. "I got raped and robbed!" She was in tears, and enraged, her body shaking in anger.

I felt terrible for my friend, but at the same time I was seeing my life go down the drain as she spoke. I really needed that money because I was behind on bills. It was looking like I wasn't going to get my cut after all. This was the exact reason why I knew I would need to advance to bigger robberies. Cash robberies. I was sick of trying to sell stolen goods. That shit was getting old and starting to become a hindrance. I knew I should have been more concerned with the well-being of my friend instead of worrying about money issues, but me and her had more of a business relationship than one about each other's well-being.

"Reecy Pooh did you go to the doctor? You don't wanna' get a rape kit?"

"Fuck a rape kit! Fuck that shit! All that shit is going to do is embarrass me. Those white people don't give a fuck about me. You know that." She yelled.

"Who did it Reecy? Shit let's go get they ass!" I screamed.

"I don't know who did it Ice! I just don't know!"

"What about Rhondo. Did you tell him what happened?" I asked.

"No." She said while wiping her tears.

"Shit well why not? You know that nigga don't play about you."

"I'm sorry Ice. I'm just so sorry! I'm sorry!" She said in a lower voice, her new tears replacing her old tears every time she wiped one.

"Call Rhondo. Call him right now Reecy."

Reecy took a deep breath and shook her head. "He's not going to give a fuck." She said.

"Call him." I said again.

I watched as she dialed Rhondo's number, not knowing what was going on between them, nor did I care. I was honestly plotting my next move.

"Rhondo... I'm sorry... I got robbed... I–"

The only reason I looked up and paid any attention to her was because she stopped talking and was sitting on the phone with a frozen face. It was obvious that Rhondo was saying some rude shit to her on the phone, but I didn't know what it was about or what she'd done to him to make him that way. I'd always known him to be head over heels in love with her.

"I wasn't trying to be sneaky in the bathroom last night Rhondo, I was only trying to do business... I–"

She didn't get a chance to get another word off. Rhondo hung up on her, leaving her looking like she was about to throw up. She sat on my sofa and put her face in her hands trying to cover her sadness. "I really fucked up Ice. I let everybody down. I don't have any money to pay my bills, I'm just down and out right now."

I walked out of the living room to go to my safe. I never touched my safe, ever, but I knew Reecy Pooh didn't save shit and she really would be fucked up without any money. I needed her to be ok while I figured out how to introduce my robbery ideas to her. I was putting the safe back when Reecy walked in my bedroom.

"Ice where is the bathroom?" She asked as I closed the secret compartment.

I pointed to my bulletin board with my bank robbery plans on it. I had it nailed against the bathroom door.

"What is all this girl? What the hell you doing? Hold on, lemme use the bathroom because we got some catching up to do."

I sat on the bed waiting on her to come out of the bathroom. She sat on the bed beside me. "Talk to me Ice. What's up?"

I was nervous about introducing my plans to her, but I knew that if I couldn't tell her, then I couldn't tell anybody. "Reecy Pooh, I'm tired of hitting these stores and shit. I'm tired of doing double the work. We have to steal the shit and then sell the shit later. I just feel like if we're going to do all that work then we might as well open our own jewelry store. At least we'll make more money for the items we steal and re-sell."

"So you want us to open a jewelry store?" Reecy asked with a frown on her face.

Ice shook her head. "No. I want us to rob a bank. I want us to rob a got damn gold mine. I want my licks to be on national news, and not swept under the rug like a petty crime. I want my robberies to be studied and I wanna go down as one of the best who ever did it."

"You just wanna' be able to make the news? I thought the goal was to stay under the radar so that we don't go to prison?" Reecy asked.

I was beginning to get angry because it felt as if she was judging me. "The goal is to be able to get money and have money instead of getting robbed trying to sell shit after we've put in work to steal the shit."

"Wow, that hurt Ice. I'm sorry I'm not so perfect. I'm sorry I don't have a working man giving my last dollar to buy my items like some people. I don't have any loyal people cutting grass to buy my shit."

"Wow really? I told you about that man so long ago that I forgot I even told you. So obviously you've been in your feelings about me for some reason? And to think I was trying to help you!" I said, hurt.

I turned away and took a deep breath, then felt Reecy's arms wrap around me, hugging me. "Girl we don't need to be arguing. We're like sisters. I wasn't trying to downplay your ideas, I just thought that what we had already was pretty damned good compared to other people out here who go to prison every day."

"We are great at what we do. That's why I believe it's time for us to elevate our hustle. If we can be good at the next level of hustling just one time... We'd be rich for years to come, especially if we manage our money correctly."

Reecy Pooh nodded her head. "Yea I guess you're right Ice. I'd have to give it some thought though. That's a big change from stealing out of stores. Let me think about it."

That's all I could really ask from her is for her to think about it.

"Well here, I know you got robbed, but here's some money until we figure out what we're going to do next about money. Go ahead and pay your bills Reecy Pooh. We're going to be straight."

Reecy hugged me so tight that I thought she was trying to suffocate me. I smiled. I knew we had our disagreements at times, but she was the only person I'd ever trusted in my life other than Ms. Lattis. I handed her the money and she put it in her purse. I knew she probably didn't wanna' rob a bank, but I really couldn't blame her for thinking like that. It wasn't like we couldn't go steal whatever we wanted out of the malls, jewelry stores and convenience stores. Me wanting to do something bigger was more out of my personal urge than necessity. I still was hoping that she could see it the way I did though.

MS. LATTIS

Sweat had been pouring out of my body the entire morning. Everything in my house reminded me of crack cocaine. I couldn't walk past the stove without imagining the heat of the fire. I couldn't turn on the microwave without hearing the sizzle of the cocaine being cooked and inhaled. I couldn't look out the window without wanting to have my old life back before Ice saved me. I'd done right by Ice, and she'd done right by me, and at this point, I didn't feel like I owed her much else.

I sat in the living room and lit a cigarette. It had been months since I smoked a cigarette, but I really needed it at that point. I needed anything that would calm me down and get the hardcore drug out of my mind. The only problem was that it wasn't working. The more I smoked the cigarette, the more I got angry that it wasn't as powerful as other drugs. I got tired of it and put it out.

"Henrietta." I heard a voice whisper.

What the fuck? I was hearing shit. There was nobody in my house and I knew it.

"Henrietta." The voice repeated. It was Otis' voice. I hadn't felt his spirit that strong in years. It never happened to me unless I had that same recurring dream again. I closed my eyes trying to trap the tears from seeping out, but it was to no avail. I sat on the sofa crying while the cigarette continued to burn in the ash tray. The walls felt like they were caving in, and the sofa felt like it was trying to help the walls keep me in place. I needed a relief, a break, a hit...

But I couldn't. I had to do something different. I couldn't relapse at this age because it would kill me and Ice too. The sound of crack being pressed by the highest volumes of fire echoed through my brain, causing my mouth to dry up and my throat to twitch. A pain shot rippled up starting at the depths of my stomach, and turned to euphoric happiness by the time it reached my brain. I wanted it so bad that it hurt, but it would hurt worse to let Ice down after she's really put her life on the line for mine.

I closed my eyes, praying the feeling would go away. "Henrietta." I heard Otis call out from that space between death and afterlife.

"What?" I answered him, a sudden pain shooting through my chest.

"Why did you leave me at the bank?"

My teeth rattled against each other, and I felt like I was on a roller coaster ride. I held on to the couch as the room started spinning, forcing me to open my eyes. It was Otis I saw in front of me, and then he disappeared, and the room slowly came to a halt. My lungs were refusing to work, and the more I tried to breathe, the more they were determined to not let me get any air.

I pushed and pushed, trying to get my lungs to working, but it was feeling like they were glued shut. My neck turned side to side and I was about to punch my chest when a gust of air cycloned through my body. I could finally breathe again.

I leaned over and threw up as my body tried to process the oxygen that my body had been deprived of. I had a migraine and a stomach ache at the same time. I got up to go get the Porsche keys.

I was going to have to do something to fix my misery, and fast. I could no longer sit there and let the world attack me. Otis felt like I left him in the bank to die, and I never wanted him to feel that way. I loved him like no other, and wanted to be with him for the rest of my life.

The FBI had been looking for me at a certain point of my life, but my next few years after that robbery went by ultra fast with me being on crack cocaine, and boosting shit on the daily basis to be able to afford my addiction. I'd been living under a rock since then, not the one I preferred, but the one that Ice preferred. For some reason, she knew I would rather be sheltered than out in the open, and she made sure to make that happen for me.

I wasn't going to put Ice through the madness again. I was going to go to the liquor store, buy a bottle of Hennessy, and be done with it. Alcohol would at least numb the pain for me, until my body could get strong enough to process the pain without it. I got the keys and walked out of the house to jump in the Porsche.

RHONDO

Sometimes even though women have good intentions, those intentions could come across in a bad way. All of the times that Reecy Pooh had attempted to help me re-learn the basics, and had attempted to help me recover through my ordeal, I'd always pushed her away from me. It may have been a mental thing that us as men go through. We never want to seem weak from someone who once only viewed us as powerful, so instead of embracing the assistance that we may need, we push them away.

Days had gone by since I'd last talked to Reecy Pooh, and it was a good thing, because I was finally able to start getting her completely out of my system. Rosina had been helping me do the things that Reecy had attempted to do, but the difference with Rosina was... I was actually doing the things. I guess a part of me knew that I couldn't fuck up with Rosina, because then I wouldn't have anybody left who would fuck with me on that level.

She'd been cooking for me, cleaning me, helping me bathe, helping me work out, helping me with my repetition of the basics... Shid she was everything that a man could ask for. Being in her company, I was able to feel my body get stronger, and my memory start to sharpen. Rosina knew she wasn't my main chick, so it seemed like the things that she was doing were done in order to secure a potential position in the future.

Hell I couldn't even get mad because she was playing her role better than any woman in my life at that moment.

I was laying back on the bed doing my homework. The task at hand was for me to read a book and answer some questions regarding some of the details that I'd read. Reading comprehension had been very difficult for me after the shooting, but since then it got increasingly easier for me. I went through the homework with ease and lay back against the pillow enjoying the coolness of the room.

Rosina walked in with a plate of fried chicken, macaroni and cheese, steamed broccoli and cornbread. She put the plate on the nightstand and smiled at me.
"Baby you know I'm not really hungry right?" I asked her while returning her smile.

"I know baby... You always tell me you're not hungry, but you always eat it."

She was right though. If she would have asked me if I was hungry, I would have told her I'm not no matter how much I was starving. I had no idea why I was like that, but I was.

"You're a real special woman Rosina. I'm thankful to have ya' in my life. Shit I don't know what I would have done without ya' fine ass."

Her Spanish cheeks flushed red. She started fidgeting her fingers like she did any time I made her nervous.

"I love you papi." She said without even looking at me.

I smiled. "Look at me when you talk to me baby."

She turned slowly, looked at me for a split second, and burst out into another smile. She turned away again.

"Oh really? You can't even look at me without being all giggidy?" I joked.

"Stop. Haha. You're making me blush for real papi."

The more I spent time with Rosina, the more my feelings were starting to develop for her. It took me to see everything she brought to the table for me to stop worrying about how her feet looked during her walk to the table.

"I'm making you blush... and you're making me fall in love..." I said absentmindedly.

Rosina stopped smiling and turned back to stare at me in awe. Her mouth was wide open and her arms were shaking frantically. Her eyes began to get moist and her lips started twitching.

"You really mean that?" She asked nervously.

"Mean what?" I had no idea what the issue was, or why she was acting like that.

"Do you really mean what you said? You know... that I'm making you fall in love with me?"

I still didn't see what the big deal was. "Of course I meant what I said baby. You've been everything I could ever ask for in a woman, and I'm really dumb for not being able to see this a long time ago."

"Wow." She said enthusiastically. "You really don't know how good it feels for me to hear you say that. It's not common for men to appreciate women these days. Men don't keep it real with women no matter how good the woman is to them... And I appreciate you Rhondo, just for telling me those words. You never know what mental battles people endure on a day to day basis, and you just really comforted me and made me feel like I was doing something right."

I was taken aback at her reaction. I never would have thought she would feel like that just based on me saying that to her. I honestly was under the impression that she had so many men chasing her, that she heard that being said to her every couple of days. That was another reason I only wanted her as a side chick. How the hell could a fine ass Spanish chick be faithful in Atlanta?

"Rosina, I always thought you had a boyfriend of some sorts. How could a beautiful woman like you not be married? How could you not be faced with temptation on a daily basis?"

She sat beside me and held my head. "Is that what you thought this whole time Rhondo? That because people are after me that I have to be after them? Well I guess you're right... Because I've been after you this entire time, and I'm still here. If you give me permission Rhondo... I'll never go no where, and I mean that on my soul. I know you..."

I fell into a trance while she continued to talk.

I couldn't believe my ears. The opportunity to have a bad ass foreign-flavored woman in my life who was going to really be down with me was right in front of me. It sounded interesting, but I had a fetish for black women with fat asses and I couldn't deny that. I still thought about Reecy Pooh, and wondered if she'd suffered enough without me. I wondered how she would treat me if I went home and walked through the door like nothing had ever gone wrong. She'd probably think she's seen a ghost.

I imagined how her body reacted when I hit her from the back. How she liked to be choked while I slid my dick through her tight, wet, tunnel.

"Baby did you hear me?" Rosina asked, breaking me out of my trance.

"I'm sorry baby. You know the medicine be having me in a zone sometimes. What did you say?" I asked, not hearing anything she'd said for the past minute straight.

"I said I can get you a job papi. I can get you out of the streets and help you level up." Rosina said innocently.

"Out the streets?" I frowned at her. My phone rang just as I was asking her that question. "Excuse me, let me take this call please." I said to her, admiring the shape of her body as she walked away.
"Yo what's up Rhondo?"

It was Stats. "What's up? What's good Stats?"

"Shit nun. Tryna' pull up on ya' to see how you doin' homey. Where ya' at?"

I froze in place without responding. I couldn't answer his question, because for some reason, his direct tone made me feel as though I couldn't trust him. That was the first time I ever felt like that towards Stats, and I didn't know why or when I started developing those thoughts. That was a very odd feeling for someone I'd been knowing since a child.

"Shit, I'm out and about right now homey."

"Where at? I'ma pull up."

"Running around, no stationary place... I'm really tryna' handle all these situations out here in the streets since I've been able to move around a little bit more. I'll hit you when I get settled in at the spot." I answered him suspiciously. I wasn't feeling Stats right then, and definitely didn't want him knowing where I laid my head at.

"Aight cool. I got some money for you from that thing you wanted me to do. Where you want me to bring it?" Stats asked.

What the fuck was wrong with that nigga? I hung the phone up on him, then I powered my phone completely off. I sat there wondering if he was trying to set me up or if he was just being stupid on the telephone.

"Baby, telephone!" Rosina screamed.

I frowned. Who the fuck could be calling me on my side bitch's phone?

"Who is it Rosina?" I asked once she walked back in the room.

"I don't know papi." She said as she handed me the phone.

"Hello? Who is this?" I asked irritated.

"Hey bro. I think your phone hung up on me."

"Stats? What the fuck? How—" Before I could get another sentence out, he hung the phone up on me. I was angry, and I took that as a warning. I knew I wasn't feeling that nigga for a reason, my intuition served me correct. Suddenly I wandered if he was the one behind my attack.

"Is everything ok papi?" Rosina asked.

"Yea..." I lied. "How did that nigga get your number?" I asked her.

"I don't know... I thought you gave it to him."

"Aight... Check this out... For the next 7 days I want you to go twice as hard helping me get back in shape. I need to be walking and moving around in the next week. Can you promise to do your best in helping me train?"

"I got you papi. I won't let you down."

PATRON

I stood in the shower fully dressed. I'd been in the shower 10 minutes and still had on my boots and jail house uniform. I'd heard the rumors and I wasn't going out like that. My cellmate told me that some niggas was going to try to rape me during my shower. The water was on and I stood there allowing the water to soak into my clothes and boots.

My entire life I'd been a working man, determined not to be a statistic, and yet here I was in the belly of the beast determined to protect myself at all costs. I wasn't going to let them kill me in here.

Most of these niggas were just angry at their own lives and wanted to make other people's lives miserable also so they could feel better. That seemed to be the way of the government also. I hated the fact I was unable to fight the FBI.

They basically told me that if I wasn't going to tell on Ice, that I would have to do time for the theft of hundreds of thousands of dollars' worth of items. That was stupid to me considering the fact that they didn't find any evidence that I'd taken shit. It was even dumber considering the fact that they really knew who did it, and were still going to make me do time for it. I knew at that point they really didn't give a fuck about me, or us as a people.

They took a working man off of the streets. Took my business from me, my life, my sanity... They knew that if I were to testify that the lady would be guaranteed to be convicted since I had such a clean record and was such a pillar in the community. I would never let them treat me like a puppet. I didn't work for nobody else when I wasn't locked up, so I wasn't about to be locked up and work for them no matter how much time they were threatening me with.

After about 15 minutes, I determined that that rumor must have been a lie. I was going to go ahead and take my shower and get the fuck out of there. I took my shirt off and tossed it on the top of the stall door. As soon as I unfastened my belt buckle, my door opened and two niggas pushed their way inside the stall. One pushed me against the opposite end of the small shower stall and the other turned to lock the door.

These men were bigger than me, but I was prepared for it. I picked my knife of and started swinging.

"Ahhhhhhh!" I stabbed the first nigga with so much power that I thought I'd broken my knife. He hit the ground shaking, and I picked my knife up and slung it into his back. He had his pants halfway down so I picked the knife up again and literally tore him a new asshole.

I didn't even recall when the other man ran out of the cell, but I recalled what he looked like. I ran out of the cell, paranoid, running around like a chicken with his neck cut off. I was looking right, left, high, low for that bastard. The cells had open doors, and I was about to go find him no matter what. I ran down the hall of the control unit looking in every cell. I was hunting because they'd tried to hunt me.

I saw him a few cell doors down, getting ready to climb in his bunk like nothing had happened. I didn't give a fuck. I ran up on him and tried to cut his entire fucking calf muscle off.

He hit the ground, blood spurt across the room, across the floor. My clothes were bloody, my body was bloody from both of the guys DNA.

"You wanted to try to rape me nigga!? Huh nigga? Huh muthafucka?" I screamed. I was out of control and didn't give a fuck! I'd just stay in prison forever if that's what I gotta do to keep my manhood! I'm a muthafuckin man, period! A boss! Not no lame. I picked my knife up above his head getting ready to kill his ass when I felt a burning electric stab go through my body, knocking me to the floor.

The guards had tased me, rendering my body damned near useless. I could barely move a muscle after being tased, and then they did it again.

"Ouuuuch!" Shit that hurt. They picked me up and slammed me on my face and then elbowed me on the top of the head. I was unconscious.

***

That night they threw me in solitary confinement, and the following day I was taken to a room where I had an attorney phone call waiting on me.

"Hello." I said, still in shock and in a daze from them tasing me the night before.

"Hey. Attorney Samuel Jenkins here. How are you?"

"I'm doing as best as I can be considering the circumstances."

"I certainly understand that sir. Well look, I'll get down to the bottom of this phone call... The government wants to offer you a chance to testify on the girl, and they said they'll let you go free. I've verified this and gotten it in writing from the prosecution, so it's not a fluke. I mean literally if you tell me you're testify against her, and you sign this paper, all of this stuff will be over with."

"What are my other options?" I asked.

"Well... your other options are to wait around and pray that those two people you stabbed last night don't die. Then you'll be charged with double murder on top of this charge you'll have to take for this woman. You know... the government doesn't want you. You understand this right? I mean... they wanted to give you 10 years for the theft ring charge alone, so if those two men die, then the next plea deal they offer you would be life."

"I'm not interested."

"In doing life? I know you're not. That's why I'm urging you to sign this paper and go home!"

"I'm not signing shit. I'll face the music however I need to."

"Oh my God. You're really telling me that you wanna gamble with the FEDs? You're silly. Clearly you're not a criminal, just some guy who ended up in a shitty situation. I'll put it like this... This deal they're offering you is so good, that if you don't sign this today, then I'm walking away from your case, period."

I dropped the phone on the desk, since the handcuffs they had on me wouldn't allow me to hang it up properly, and two guards came and escorted me back into solitary confinement.

REECY POOH

I'd been calling Rhondo's phone all week and he'd been sending me straight to voicemail. I hated that because all I was trying to do was check on him to make sure he was alright. I didn't want him not being able to take care of himself and have nobody around to look after him. I'd been going by the house every day to see if he was there, but he wasn't. I called his number again every day, all day, and still got no answer.

Finally one day I gave in and called Stats trying to see if he would answer for me. To my surprise he answered on the second ring.

"Stats. Hey... This is Reecy Pooh."

"Hey hey. What's up? Is Rhondo there?" He asked.

"Nah, hell I was hoping to ask you that same question."

"Ohhh... Aight." He said. "He must still be with that Rosina chick."

What? "What muthafuckin' Rosina bitch?" I screamed into the phone. "Who the fuck is that?"

"Some bitch I heard he's staying with. I've been looking for her house though because something ain't right with Rhondo."

I had a confused look on my face. "What you mean something ain't right nigga? Something like what?" I was baffled.

"Well, I heard he gave the police some information that he shouldn't have, and that's the reason the nigga tried to kill him last time."

"What kind of information Stats?" I was nervous at that point. I had a few skeletons in my closet too...

"Shit I heard some detectives were at y'all house one day. And after that, it was like... a bunch of our niggas started getting locked up. Even the plug got locked up and we had to switch to another nigga. Then now... the cops been following me and him too. Where were you when the cops came by? What did they want? Do you remember?" He asked.

"Didn't no cops come by my house Stats." I said nonchalantly.

"Shittin me! One of my lil' niggas was headed over there for me and he ended up taking pictures! I got the pictures to prove it!"

Shit! I was panicking. More so because I was starting to realize that Rhondo getting shot was all my fault. *Oh my God, what have I done?* I thought to myself.

"I'm sure it has to be a misunderstanding Stats." I said, my heart beating fast as hell.

I thought back to the day those cops came by the house almost 18 months ago. They were about to arrest me for theft that day, but instead they agreed to let me go if I could tell them the vehicle tag numbers of the next 5 people who came by to visit Rhondo, no matter who it was. I wasn't going to do it but they promised that nothing was going to happen to Rhondo. They promised it had nothing to do with him and that me and Ice would continue to be free. They told me if I didn't do it, they would lock up Rhondo, me, and Ice too. I *had* to do it.

"Stats I don't believe my man is a snitch. Period." I said, quickly wondering how I could find him to tell him what was going on.

"Well you can believe what you want, but that ain't gon' stop the streets from killing him. And since I've told you... then you know you're at risk too. I'm letting you know in advance, but these niggaz ain't bout to play with y'all out here in these streets Reecy."

I was pacing back and forth wishing I could fix my mistakes to at least stop them from killing me or Rhondo. I was angry that he was with another bitch, but at the same time I felt guilty for being the reason that he got shot in the first place. I started feeling like I had to throw up, but I was able to hold it. I grinded my teeth and closed my eyes for a second.

"How much money would it take to fix it Stats?" I asked.

"Shit... It's gon take some real paper to fix Reecy. I'm talking about the type of real paper that you don't have... Didn't you just get robbed by Jiip and Al the other day?"

"Huh? Fuck no! Somebody came in and robbed me, Jiip, and killed Al."

"You trippin Reecy Pooh. I'm talmbout tripping real fuckin hard. Albert's lil bad ass is still alive. Jiip is out here stunting and shit. You done fucked around and got *got!*"

His words echoed in my head. I was the maddest I had ever been in my life! *That nigga raped and robbed me and then tried to fuckin play me. I'ma kill that nigga if it's the last fuckin thing I do.*

"Yea... well... I still can get some money from Ice. She got a lil stash left. So just let me know how much it's going to take to fix this shit in the streets." I said, wondering how I was going to convince Ice to let me borrow her stash to save my life.

"Shit say no more Reecy Pooh. I'll relay the message."

Jiip

My last few licks had gone so good, that I decided to actually start *buying* shit. I'd just purchased at blue 2017 Range Rover, and I was having a good time shittin' on the hood. Me and Albert had turned out to be a helluva team, and there was no lick we couldn't hit, and no situation we couldn't finesse our way out of. I liked that young nigga, and I knew that we were going to raise hell on the streets for years to come.

We had a pattern that we followed every few days. I would always drop him off in the hood and let him flirt with them young ass bitches who would tell him all the pillow talk. Then I would pick him up at the end of the day, and most times I be knowing every thing about every got damn body. Shit just worked like that in the hood, nobody knew how to keep their mouth shut, and there was no such thing as a secret.

I picked him up off of Bankhead that evening, and waved at a few of the niggas I knew who were hanging out at the barbershop.

"What's up young nigga?" I said once he closed the door.

"Shit coolin' Unc. Shit slow motion today, got some small news though, nun' major."

"Don't sweat it, we'll chop it up in detail when we get back to the spot." I said while turning that new Ralo Laflare mixtape back up. I liked his shit because I could hear the *threat* in his voice. I'm talking about the same type of threat that I carried when I went to hit a lick, and only a nigga who was a professional lick-hitter could understand that threat.

"Nah Unc. You might wanna' hear this shit now. This one of them situations that we can get fixed before even making it to the spot." He spoke loud over the music.

I turned the music down. "What's up nephew? Shid talk to me."

"I heard from that nigga Stats, that that bitch we robbed been staying with her friend Ice. Shid... I heard the bitch Ice got a real stash spot over in the hood. I been calling my young niggas over that way and they said the bitch been gone all day. You can drop me off like a pizza and I'll bring that lil' stash back."

"Fuck that. I'ma wait on you. The fuck I look like dropping you off so you can get rich? We in route right now. I think I know the bitch you talmbout too. Shit text me the address and say less lil' nephew."

I turned the GPS on, eager to hit this lick. "Aye look... I been thinking Al... Shid... if we can get a big enough lick, we can just take over the dope game round this bitch. I like taking shit from these niggas, but have you ever noticed how much money it be when we be hitting these dope boy stash spots and shit? We need to stop them niggaz from eating. I mean... We sitting on a nice amount of money right now, so imagine if the whole city became ours? I know you got some young niggas you can put in position right?"

"Hell yea shid. I was just bought to tell you that Unc. It's a bunch of niggas lookin fa' somebody to lead them. They ain't gon follow nobody who ain't got no work. Shid if we can get enough work, we gon' own the streets. I'm down for whatever Unc, that's on everything."

ICE

I spent my entire day driving around Atlanta looking at bank set-ups. The way I saw shit... I wasn't gon' be able to get nobody to fuck with me on the bank robberies, so I was gon' have to do the shit myself. I didn't have time to be selling no more fuckin' watches. Out here risking my life two times for the same damn dollar. Niggas wasn't working that hard after stealing shit. It would be easier if we had people already in place to buy the shit, but we had to risk our lives again to find niggas who wouldn't rob our ass.

I'd cased a few Wells Fargo branches, checked out a PNC location in Buckhead, and another one downtown by Georgia Tech, looked into robbing the Brand Bank in Buckhead off the main street, and even checked out the PNC bank in the grocery store off of Cleveland. My mind was frazzled, and I was tired as hell. When I went around these banks, I started feeling like these banks could be a potential waste of time too.

What if I robbed a bank and only left out with $40,000 cash? That shit was not going to cut it. I can steal a few watches and wait on $40,000 without risking going to prison on some high level shit.

Fuck the banks. I thought as I pulled up to my apartment that night. It was almost midnight and I was just making it home. I knew I was going to be up a few more hours studying the internet to learn more about robberies. I knew the ins and outs, the consequences and pitfalls like the back of my hand at that point, but it was never a such thing as learning too much. The more I was able to absorb, the better off I would be.

When I walked into the house, it looked like a hurricane had run through it.

What the fuck?

My sofa was flipped upside down and there was a knife cut ripped through it. My cabinets were open and cereal boxes were dumped inside out. My refrigerator had been moved, my closets were wide open... and I realized what had happened.

I quickly ran to my stash box, and that muthafucka was gone.

I bit my lip, my fists squeezed shut, and anger ripped through my body. I ran to my bed to see if my pistol was under it, but it was gone too. The only person in the world who knew about my stash box was Reecy Pooh, and *that* was by accident– *only* because she walked in when I was trying to help her ass. I couldn't believe she would steal from me when I was only tryna' help her. That really hurt my feelings to the core.

I picked my phone up and called her line, hoping for some type of explanation. I needed to know why she would do me like that. I walked outside and sat in the car while the phone rang.

"Hello. Hey Ice." She finally answered.

"Reecy. What's going on?"

"A whole lot is going on Ice. I really need your help! Can you let me borrow some more money? I don't know how much I'm going to need, but I'm sure it's going to be a lot. I've fucked up even more than before Ice. I really have to tell you this in person."

I felt myself burning inside. "Why the fuck would you take my money and then ask me to borrow the shit after the fact man? That's so fuckin' disrespectful Reecy! I thought we were better than that! We stole from everyone else, not each other!"

"What? Oh my God, I would never steal shit from you Ice! I need you to know that! You're the only friend I have right now! Why would I–"

I hung the phone up on her. I didn't wanna hear that shit. What was the use of sitting there letting her try to convince me of a lie? My fuckin money was gone. All the money I had ever put aside from all of my work in... she'd came and taken it from me during my weakest moments. I sat back in the seat and tried to get a hold of myself to figure out my next move. I no longer wanted to live in that apartment, but I also didn't want to invade Ms. Lattis' space. I had a lot of thinking to do but had a limited amount of time to do the thinking.

Jiip

"You understand what I mean by *taking* shit even when you can just walk away with it?" I asked Al. I was trying to teach him what it meant to be a real savage in these streets. It was too many weak ass niggas, and I didn't want him to be one.

"I understand Unc."

"Good. Because if we wouldn't have waited in this parking lot, we would have left ourselves vulnerable for payback. We don't want payback after stealing this bitch's stash. We want that ho dead! Ain't no playing around. We don't do no fuck boy robberies, we do the real deals. Everything must go like that shit on sale!"

"Helllll yea! I feel that Unc. Shit I'm ready to take some shit right now!"

"That's the spirit Al. Aight I'ma drive my truck close to where she's sitting at in the car, and you spray that muthafucka up! You ready?"

"I'm ready Unc. Let's go!"

ICE

I was sitting in the car trying to gather my thoughts when a blue Range Rover pulled up beside me on my driver side. I looked in the two men's faces thinking they were about to try to holla' at me when the younger looking one on the passenger side pulled up an automatic rifle with a drum on the bottom and aimed it at me.

"Shit!" I slid the car into gear and slammed my foot on the gas as hard as possible.

"Shoot that bitch! What's your prob–"

I didn't hear another word because I was gone. I ran the stop sign and flew through traffic going 70 miles and hour and jumped straight on the expressway. I checked my rear view but didn't see them following me, but that didn't mean I was going to slow down. I increased my speed to 100 miles an hour, and almost lost control of my little Honda, but I held it down.

I tried to grab my phone to call Reecy Pooh, but it slipped out of my hand and landed on the floor of the passenger seat.

"Shit! Fuck it."

I kept driving until I got to Ms. Lattis' place. I parked my car and ran up the stairs to her door. I didn't usually pop up at her place that late at night, but this situation was certainly an emergency. I knocked on the door and rang the doorbell, waiting on her to open up. My mind was racing thinking about all of the events of the day. I had crammed in so many elements in a 12-hour period. I'd cased banks, comforted a rape and robbery victim, been robbed, had someone to try to kill me, and here I was at Ms. Lattis' spot at near midnight.

When I noticed that about 7 minutes had gone by, I figured that she was probably sleep. I would have just come back the next day, but I really needed to talk to someone I trusted, even if for a few minutes. I grabbed my keychain, located the extra key I had to her place and unlocked the door. I locked the door back behind me and almost fainted when I saw Ms. Lattis slumped over at the kitchen table.

"Henrietta!" I screamed.

She jumped up, startled. "Sugar you scared me! What you doin' over here this time of night?" Ms. Lattis yelled at me, a funny look on her face.

"What you doing slumped over at the table like that?" I asked, looking around the kitchen for anything that didn't need to be there. It seemed to be clean, and I didn't want to offend her by assuming or falsely accusing her of anything. It wasn't the time for all that.

"Sugar I fell asleep, that's all. I'm about to get in the bed now that you woke me up, but what's up with you? What's wrong baby?"

It's funny that I'd drove all the way to Ms. Lattis' house just to have a conversation with her about everything that had happened, and now that I was in front of her, I'd changed my mind. Something didn't feel right about the vibe. It felt like she had some problems and issues that she was going through and I didn't want to bother an older lady with young lady problems. I simply needed to grow up and fix my situations so that I can be better as a person.

"Nothing is wrong Ms. Lattis. I was simply in the area after handling some business in the area, and I wanted to make sure you were ok." I lied.

"I'm fine." She said fidgeting with her fingers. I could tell she was lying, but I didn't know what the truth was, so I had nothing to compare it to in argument. I looked in her face and noticed that her eye balls looked bigger than normal, but I figured maybe it was because I'd just woke her ass up at midnight. A random wake up may have done that to her eyes, and I suddenly felt bad for even barging in on her like that. She deserved her privacy as much as the next person, and I was determined to give her that.

"Well I'll see you tomorrow Ms. Lattis. Be good, be safe, and when I get here tomorrow we'll sit down and I'll tell you everything that's going on with me."

"O.K. sugar," Ms. Lattis said as she walked up behind me to close the door.

I stopped once she got closer to me. I smelled an odor coming from her that I'd smelled before— but I couldn't pinpoint what that fragrance was specifically. It was getting late and my brain was getting tired, so I was going to have to get to the bottom of things the next day. In the meantime, I just needed to get to a nice hotel room so that I could get some sleep.

I took a step outside of her door and turned around and looked at her one last time. "Have you been drinking Ms. Lattis?" I asked her, trying not to sound accusatory, just wanted to ease my thoughts.

"Yea some of that good ol' sweet tea!" She started laughing. "Gone and get you some rest sugar." She said as she closed and locked her door.

I was going to use one of my credit cards and book a room at the Mandarin Oriental for the night. Sleep was certainly calling my name.

Jiip

"What the fuck happened Al? Why didn't you kill that bitch? She saw our faces and everything and you still let the ho live? What's up with that?" I was pissed at his young dumb ass for pulling that stunt. I'd just sat there and gave his stupid ass a speech on what it meant to take some shit, and his lame ass had the nerve to just take his stupid ass time.

"I pulled the trigger Unc. Ain't shit come out this muthafucka!" Albert said while throwing his hand up in defeat.

"Gimme that gun nigga. Fuck you talmbout?"

He handed me the gun and I looked at the drum, realizing my fuck up. "Oh damn lil nephew. My fault." I shook my head and sighed.

"What happened Unc?"

"This is one I just got custom-made earlier. This drum holds 200 bullets. I picked it up from the Russians earlier. I handed you the wrong one. The one that's fully loaded and ready to go is in the backseat on the floor. Damn that's my fault lil homey."

"It's ok Unc. I'ma let her have it whenever I see her, I promise."

"Nah, chill nephew. You'll have plenty opportunity to learn how to *take* shit in the future. That bitch ain't nobody. I mean literally nobody. We bout to have all this dope in the streets, so it's time to start moving different. Tonight was our last time taking shit or trying to take shit, and from here on out we'll send our soldiers and workers to handle our dirty work. We gotta start moving like bosses now."

"I'm with it Unc." Albert said as he smiled.

"That's why I fucks with you nephew." The bond we shared was stronger than father and son, and that's why I had so much love for the up and coming street celebrity.

ICE

I only slept for a few hours at the Mandarin Oriental hotel. It had been my routine to study robberies and learn more about them from Youtube, and through searching details from the internet for years, and that was the first time I'd gone to bed without my research.

I woke up in the middle of the night with a burning desire to learn more. I pulled up an armored truck robbery case from Los Angeles where both of the potential robbers got killed on the scene. The common factor in all of these cases failing was the fact that these robbers don't go in with the intention of killing the truck drivers. Nearly all of them have it in their minds that this is going to be just a peaceful ol' robbery. Give me the money and keep your hands up type of shit.

Armored trucks were far from peaceful. The companies in charge of shipping large sums of funds weren't about to have their reputations weakened, and definitely weren't about to let other criminals think shit was sweet. They made sure to have their workers trained to kill. There was no negotiating, only firepower. Transporting millions of dollars at a time was a severely nerve wrenching job, but it had to be done. Stores made so much money through the day, and even more in a week's time, and all of this cash had to find it's way to the banks securely.

I was writing details on a particular company, Loomis, who considered themselves a cash management company. Just by searching all of the details of their website, looking at their videos and brochures, I was able to make my decision on how I wanted to go about things. I didn't feel like I would be able to take them out alone however, so I would definitely have to figure out the best route to go about things.

I thought back to the guy's face who wanted to kill me earlier, and I wondered if that was the same guy who'd stolen my stash. I hated the fact that they'd taken everything I'd worked for, but I couldn't be angry about it though. I'd been stealing shit for years, and I knew that eventually what goes around comes around. I still wasn't going to let that stop me from grinding though.

My phone rang, just as I was writing my last idea regarding Loomis cash management procedures.

"Hello?"

"Ice I'm sorry. I truly am, but just know I had nothing to do with your stash coming up stolen. I really didn't do it." Reecy Pooh's voice was ragged from crying all night. She really wanted Ice to trust her. That was the only friend she had, literally.

"Oh I believe you Reecy."

"Thank God! Ice I'm willing to help you find whoever robbed you. I got two of the guns Rhondo left at the house, and they each hold like 30 bullets at a time. I'll bring you one and we can hit these streets to get your money back. I'm with whatever."

Ice used that opportunity to bring back up her original idea.

"If you're with whatever like you say you are, then let's hit a bank Reecy."

Reecy hesitated for a minute. She sighed. "You know what Ice... I'm really against that, but if it'll make you happy, then I'll rob whatever the fuck it is you wanna rob. I'm with you for real and I mean that."

Ice smiled. She was bubbling in happiness from Reecy agreeing to rob a bank with her, but she actually had other plans. "Thank you for that Reecy. But I only said the bank to test you out to see if you would roll with me."

Reecy exhaled. "Oh thank goodness you don't wanna hit a bank. That would have been so dangerous."

"Nah, we gon step it up a notch Reecy Pooh. We gon hit a Loomis truck. Pull up on me, matter fact... meet me at Ruth's Chris up in Buckhead."

"A Loomis truck? Them drivers be strapped like them kids backs on the first day of scool! What the fuck? You just plan on having a straight up shootout in the middle of the broad day?"

"What the fuck Reecy? How you gon' tell me that you're down for whatever and yo' Trina lookin ass can't even fuck with me on some shit I really wanna do? Think of all the shit you've wanted me to do and I was against, and I still did the fuck shit. Why can't you also be a friend to me? Fuck with me the way I fuck with you!" I was getting beyond angry. I didn't understand why I had to convince her ass to rock with me. I really thought we were better than that.

Reecy sighed. "Aight Ice. I'm with you. What time you want me to meet you at Ruth's Chris?"

PATRON

I'd been in solitary confinement for almost three weeks at that point. They kept me in the cell 23 hours a day, and let me out for an hour to shower and walk around the "yard," which was nothing but a small cement square with a fence around it. It was amazing the amount of security the government had invested into in order to keep criminals locked in a cage. I knew that if they had the money to create such a system like that, then they could also create another system that could help potential criminals get on a legit track in life and stay there.

"Patrick Smith! Lawyer visit!" The guard yelled through the speaker. I was eager to have some type of interaction, because I was beginning to go crazy in solitary confinement by myself. I hurriedly walked to the door and waited on them to hit the locks to let me out of there. The first guard walked to the door holding a notepad. He wrote down some things and looked through the slot in the cage.

"You Patrick Smith?"

"I am."

"You got your ID?"

I reached in my pocket and pulled out my cheap laminated prison ID card and showed it to him. He wrote something down and another guard walked up next to him with the keys.

"Is that him?" The one with the keys asked.

"It is, I just checked."

The door popped open and they put handcuffs on my legs and arms, and had me follow them to an elevator. We took the elevator up a floor and they led me down a hall. Another set of guards took over from there and let me to a room with a glass window inside it. I sat down on the metal stool and stared at the man in a suit on the other side of the glass.

He pointed at the black phone, and picked his up. I followed suit.

"Hello."

"Hi. My name is Attorney Brent Sanchez, and I'm your new court appointed lawyer."

"O.K." I said, I really didn't care one way or the other. I'd never been in trouble before, so I was hoping for probation.

"Well Mr. Smith... You're not in as much hot water as you were in 3 weeks ago, but you're still in a pretty tight spot right now. So the second guy you allegedly stabbed, he's made it out of his coma. He's going to testify against you. He told the government that you attacked him in cold blood."

"He tried me in the fuckin shower! The fuck you mean! I'm a man!" I screamed through the phone.

"Wait, calm down... let me tell you the rest of the bad news. The first guy you stabbed, you really did a number on him... He's not expected to make it. The good news is... since they recovered his body from the bathroom floor of the stall, your story holds up and they'll write it off as self-defense *if* you sign this plea deal."

I was starting to get angry all over again. "What? I'm not testifying on nobody man. Nobody."

"Alright... that's fine. This one is different. You don't have to testify on the girl on this one. They just wanna get this over and done with at this point. So this deal is for 5 years, but you could possibly get out in 3 years with good behavior."

I dropped my head in my palm. All I'd ever done my entire life was abide by the law, work, and take care of all of my responsibilities, and here I am in a terrible jam, no better than any common thug or any basic criminal. The worst thing about the entire scenario however, was the fact that I didn't see an error in my ways. I'd done nothing anything different than any man would do had he been faced with the same options.

I knew that had I been a white man, I would have been allowed to go right back to work with my landscaping company. The odds were laid out so unfairly in America. No matter which path you chose, you always were at risk of losing your life. Innocent drivers being killed because of their race, people being choked while in handcuffs, to the cops murdering so many people in cold blood... I just prayed that if I do the 5 years I could live through it long enough to make it home.

"If you don't sign it Mr. Smith, you run the risk of being charged if the other guy doesn't make it out of his coma. You almost had to face two of these, but luckily the first guy pulled through. Don't take this chance twice Mr. Smith."

"Gimme the paper. I'll sign it."

JOSE

When I first got locked up, and sent to the immigration unit, I was feeling bad for myself– feeling bad that my family wouldn't be able to live as good as they were when I was sending money home every week. I was getting depressed until I started listening to stories from other people who were also getting deported. I'd met a man by the name of Jerado who was in an even worse predicament than I was in. I sat in the cell on the bunk listening to him express himself.

"I was brought to Texas when I was 6 months old man. It's crazy. All I know is America. I've never even been to Mexico to visit. My entire life man, all I've ever known is the United States, and now here I am getting deported back to a place I've never even been. How could they send me somewhere I never came from? Like that's not fair to me man. I can't speak Spanish, I have no family there, I have nowhere to stay. What will I even do? How do I adjust?"

Everyone had a different set of obstacles in front of them, and after hearing so many different scenarios, I stopped feeling so bad about my own. I'd talked to my wife and she reassured me that everything was going to be just fine. She told me she'd made some really good investments with the money I'd been sending her, and that she thought I would be extremely pleased by the time I arrived.

I tried asking her on the phone what the investments were, but she insisted that it would be better if she showed me in person. That made me nervous when she first said that, but she continued to reassure me that she knew I was going to be happy about it. She knew my tastes better than anyone, so I really couldn't doubt the fact that she knew what I would like as an investment. I just had to be patient until I arrived back in Mexico.

RHONDO

Rosina really held me down when I needed her, and after a couple of weeks of intensive therapy, I was right back in the driver's seat of my life; although I didn't have a vehicle to my name. A few niggas in the streets owed me money, and I was going to try to pick up as much as I could. I borrowed Rosina's car and headed to the trap house that me and Stats were getting money from. I pulled up a half block away from the house, and saw Stats sitting on the porch talking to some niggas I'd never seen before. He was deep in a conversation so they weren't paying me any mind since I was so far away.

I picked up my phone to call him, when Reecy Pooh called my phone again. She had been calling my phone nonstop for weeks, but I hadn't answered it not one time. I was too busy getting my life together.

"Yea what's up?"

"Thank God you're ok Rhondo!" She said as if she was excited about that.

"Fuckin right I'm ok. I'm walking. Driving. Moving... Fucking. All that shit. What's good, Rhondo's back on these muthafuckin streets. Yea... All these people who fucked over me and left me for dead gon pay for this shit." I said, not meaning to vent at her like that, but unable to help it.

"Rhondo, I know you think I'm one of those people, but I'm not. I'm going to make it up to you I promise. I had to handle some real business to insure that we were able to live the way we always wanted to live. I know you think I let you down, and I know you think your lil bitch is all you need right now, but when I see you I'ma have almost a half million dollars in cash for yo' ass. Can she do that?"

Whoa. She really fucked me up with that one. I'd never had a half million dollars at once... Ever in my life. I'd been stuck in the cycle of moving petty amounts of drugs, in the ever going dream of trying to double and triple up to sell bigger amounts. That dream seemed to never happen faster than the speed of the life of the streets. I couldn't even be mad at her ass if she was finna' bring me a half million dollars.

"I guess you gon' take the other half to that fuck nigga Jiip right? Yea I heard the rumors... That was supposed to be your lil man on the side right? Meanwhile I'm getting shot outside of the jewelry shop tryna marry yo' funky ass!"

"Please don't ever bring that nigga's name up again! Fuck that nigga! I'll tell you everything when I see you, I promise. And baby listen... if you were going to marry me, don't change your mind about me because I've never changed my mind about you. I've always wanted to marry you, and I still want that life with you. I know I'ma bring you a half million dollars, but if I can bring you a whole million, please believe I'll bring that to you too. I love you."

It was hard for me not to smile while listening to her promise me amounts of money that large. Damn! A million dollars would set us straight for real! I would probably take a few hundred thousand dollars and put it back in the streets, but shit, even with $700,000 left we would still be unfuckwitable out here. I was so excited I no longer gave a fuck about Stats and whatever he had going on anymore. Fuck that nigga.

"Man... say Reecy Pooh... When will I be able to see you? When will you have that money for me? I've been ready to get out of these streets risking my life everyday. That kind of money will help us both boss up. We can get us a nice ass pad in Buckhead, way out the way of the fuck shit going on in the streets and in the hood. We can live life to the max, have us some kids, get married, have some more kids, go on big boy vacations and just be at peace with each other. We've both been through so much shit. What do you say?"

"I say hell yea Rhondo. That's all I've ever wanted from you. If you can promise me that, then the money definitely isn't an issue. I'll call you tomorrow and let you know where we can meet up at. But you have to promise me this too... Tomorrow when I give this money to you, just know that I really risked my life and integrity to get this amount of money, and I need you to protect me until it's my time to go." Reecy Pooh said somberly.

"You don't have to tell me that baby. On my soul, I'll never let a thing happen to you. You're good in my hands, and will be good until the end of time. We gon live forever. Husband and wife."

MS. LATTIS

That was a close call the night before, having Ice show up on me unexpectedly in the middle of the night. She walked in my house and I was passed out from all those shots of Hennessy I'd had yesterday. I was going through some deep emotional shit yesterday, but I was finally able to get it out of my system without me relapsing. I was in the kitchen drinking my sweet tea, waiting on Ice and Reecy Pooh to show up.

Ice had called me and told me they wanted to come over and discuss the plan they had with me, just so they could use me as a sounding board. Ice told me that she already knew I was going to be against it, but she needed me as a friend today and not as an advisor. I agreed, even though I knew it could possibly be the last time I ever saw her alive... I still needed to be a friend to her just as she was a friend to me all of those years.

Reecy Pooh actually showed up before Ice did. She had a determined look on her face, and I wanted them to get it right since Ice wanted it to happen so bad. I poured Reecy Pooh a cup of tea and she sat at the table in silence, drinking tea with me. I wanted to tell her how I was against this plan that Ice had, but I had to keep remembering that this was no longer about advice and about support.

The door opened and Ice walked in carrying a backpack and a duffle bag. She put them both down on the floor as soon as she walked in the door, and sat on the floor besides her items. Me an Reecy Pooh got up and walked over to her to see what she was doing.

"You aight Ice?" Reecy asked. "What's in that bag?"

Ice closed the door and locked it. "Ok first lemme tell you all the plan completely..."

"The Loomis armored truck facility is located here." Ice pulled out a map out of the backpack and sat it upright against the wall. "Inside of this facility is where they distribute the money into various trucks to go to various financial institutions and businesses. The common criminal waits until one of these trucks make it to Wal-Mart, or they try to catch one leaving or going to a casino, but we're not the average criminals.

The vaulted warehouse door opens right here." Ice pointed to a spot on the map. "This is the entry of this armored vehicle into ongoing traffic. You have to remember that this vehicle is bulletproof, and the drivers are trained to kill. There will be between $6 and $18 million dollars in cash in this vehicle. There is nothing bulletproof enough to stop us from collecting this level of money."

Reecy Pooh could feel her mouth start to water while thinking about how happy Rhondo was going to be when she brought him back her cut from the robbery.

"In this duffle bag is a SERBU BFG-50A. This .50 caliber weapon will knock a fucking whole straight through the bulletproof windshield, killing their ass on the spot." Ice said, excitedly.

Reecy Pooh was stunned. "Wait, we gotta kill people?" She asked.

I interjected. "Reecy Pooh maybe this operation isn't for you baby girl. I can't have nobody hesitating when it comes to my sugar. Either you gon' be with it or you ain't Reecy." I said, surprising everybody in the room.

Reecy stared at me in shock, not expecting me to say those words. "I didn't say I wasn't going to do it. That ain't no major obstacle for the amount of money involved. I'm ready to get to it and stop talking about it. Come on Ice, lets go ahead and make a move." Reecy said irritated.

Ice exhaled. "Aight so after we kill them, we have to take the entire truck, but we have to continue the normal route that the truck would normally take until we get here." Ice said pointing to another spot on the map. "I have a van parked here and ready to go, gassed up and everything. We gon unload as much of the money as we can, and it's not even going to look suspicious because this is a part of the normal route that they already take. Then after that, we gon abandon the truck, and take the van to this place."

She pointed to another spot on the map. "It's two vehicles here, and we gon split the money up and go on our way. We'll need to lay very low after this robbery Reecy Pooh. No balling out, no major purchases. We'll need to really wash our hands and act like nothing happened for quite a while. You hear me?" Ice asked.

"I hear you Ice Ice baby."

"I'm serious, stop playing Reecy Pooh."

"Nah, I'm dead ass serious. I'm ready for this shit. As ready as I would ever be in my life. Let's make it happen."

I gave both of the girls a group hug, and then looked Ice in the eyes. "Please be safe out there sugar. You know I love you right?"

"I love you too Ms. Lattis."

ICE

The guns weighed 25 pounds each, so there was no way we could hold them in the air and aim them and still have a good enough shot. Instead, we positioned ourselves on the ground in the alley way across the street, with the guns on stands so that the weight of them could be supported. The smell of the alley disgusted us both, and I could tell that some homeless people lived out there during the nights. I wonder if they ever knew how much money was literally right in front of them every single day.

Weird how the world worked. All these people starving, when meanwhile literally hundreds of millions of dollars are being hidden from their eyesight all day every day. Just like clockwork, the armored garage door let up, allowing the big armored truck to make an exit. The garage let down and the truck was waiting for a break in traffic so it could come out.

"3, 2, 1."

Pooooooow!

Click-clack.

Poooooow!

We both shot our weapons in rhythm, both hitting our targets twice. The impact of 4 rounds of bullets from a .50 caliber pistol damned near knocked the entire windshield in. We ran out of the alley, jumped in the truck, and realizing that it was going to be difficult to get the bodies out of the cabin and still stay on time, we decided to drive with the dead bodies still in there.

Reecy Pooh sat in the dead driver's lap as we drove down the street according to the map that we'd created. "Shit we did it bitch!" I said with a big smile on my face.

For the moment all was perfect in the world. There were no police officers behind us, nobody bothering us, and nothing stopping us.

We made it to the location that had the van, and started getting as much money out the back as possible. We were surprised to discover that the money was way heavier to move than the .50 caliber rifle we used, but we had to move as much of the money as we could as fast as we could. We were home free at that point. We moved a few bales of cash, and after about 8 bales, I told her we have to leave the rest of the money in the truck.

"Leave it?" Reecy Pooh looked at me like I was crazy. "Ice ain't nobody following us or even paying us any attention baby. I think we can unload the entire truck! God knows I need more money."

I sighed. "Reecy, ok, you can have 5 bales and I'll just take 3 bales of money. We got like a half million dollars in each bail, so right now we got like $2 million each. We're good! Shit you can take $2.5 million, I don't care!"

Reecy smiled. "Damn it's that much? Well shit, yea let's go then! Fuck it!"

We took off, headed to our next destination. We had made it, and gotten away scott-free. There was absolutely nobody following us, no police activity, no sirens, nothing. It was perfectly masterminded. I closed my eyes thinking about all of the sweat and countless nights I'd stayed up trying to figure out the perfect lick, all the way up to today, with the blissful emotion of the greatest lick ever flowing through my body.

"I love you girl!" Reecy Pooh screamed as she pulled up to our final destination. It really was a wonderful plan, and even I was surprised at how well we were able to pull it off.

Reecy Pooh stopped the van and smiled when she seen that I'd arranged for us to both have new Chevy Suburbans. "These are nice as hell Ice. I like this shit. You're a genius baby."

I smiled and handed her the key to her vehicle, and got out and started trying to pick up one of the bales of money to put it in the back of my Surburban. I managed to put one of them in, but had to take a break, so I leaned against the truck for a second. When I turned back around, Reecy Pooh had already put all of her bales in, leave me with two more. She wasn't joking about taking more and leaving me with less, but it was ok, it's what I agreed to. I was just happy that we didn't have do this type of work for quite a long time.

"Reecy Pooh, while you're at it, why don't you help me put my other two bails in my car? I'm so tired... I been up all night trying to get those guns for the robberies."

"Aight Ice, I'll help you. Come help me carry it." She said as she waited on me to get up and walk over there.

I got there and put my hand on the bale and she pulled a pistol on me.

My life flashed before my eyes, and I didn't understand what was going on at all. "Reecy really?" I asked while looking at her in disbelief. "Wow man. Are you fuckin serious? I mean... you didn't even WANT to do the job, AND I'm giving you more money than me, and you're STILL going to rob me? What have I ever done to you to deserve this shit man? Like for real? I've been nothing but a fuckin friend to you!"

She pressed the pistol closer to my temple and shook her head. "I never said you did anything to me Ice. I know you've been nothing but a friend to me, and this really isn't even about you honestly."

"Well what the fuck is it about? Can't we fix whatever the problem is? I mean damn why do I have to always have the worse luck when I'm nothing but a good person to everybody? Oh my God this really breaks my heart Reecy Pooh."

Tears began to fall down Reecy Pooh's face. "I gotta ask you to forgive me Ice. I really need you to understand though. I have to do this to keep my man."

"What??? Wow... You think you gotta kill me to keep a man? That's so fuckin stupid Reecy! I don't give a fuck about your man. You can let me live and still keep your damn man! What the fuck is this about?"

"I know you're saying that, but it's like this... I wanna take Rhondo all the money. Not half, not two thirds, I want him to have it all. Every piece of this $4 million I wanna walk up in there and hand to him, and I don't wanna have to look over my shoulder worrying about when you're going to come kill me. You see... This really isn't about you. I just want you to know that I'll forever love you and everything you've ever done for me. If I could do things different, I swear I would."

The sound of tire screeching made both of us turn around. My heart was already broken, and at that point I didn't even give a fuck if it was the police or not. I was defeated.

Reecy pushed me to the ground and started shooting. I took the opportunity to roll over and hide behind the Suburban as I listened to the trading sound of gunfire. Tears fell from my eyes, and I didn't even have the energy to look behind me to see what was happening. I looked in the distance and seen where I could hide behind a building. I wanted to make a dash for it, but I knew I wouldn't be able to stand up without risking being shot. Reecy's Suburban backed up and hit the van, then it shot forward and onto the highway.

She got away? She won the shoot out? I peeped under my Suburban to see how many police cars she had been shooting with, and my heart broke when I saw Ms. Lattis' Porche with the windshield shattered. What goes around came back around just that fast... The same fate we'd brought to the armed guards, was the same fate that Reecy Pooh had brought to my pride and joy... The only person I had ever cared about in my entire life... Ms. Lattis.

I ran over to the Porsche as fast as I could and opened the door.

"Mama! You ok? Mama! Talk to me!" I screamed.

A bullet had penetrated her shoulder, her arm, and her thigh, and she was loosing a lot of blood.

"Ice go! Get out of here!" Ms. Lattis yelled at me, out of breath.

"I'm not leaving you Mama! I'll never leave you! You know I'll never leave your side!"

I grabbed my phone and got ready to dial 911.

"No! Don't you dial nothing! Get the fuck out of here and take as much money as you can! Leave one bail of money over here by my truck, and this is going to set you free!" Ms. Lattis was talking crazy.

"No! I'm going to get you to the hospital!" I tried to call 911 again and she spit on me.

"You need to fuckin listen to me Ice!" She was clearly pissed. "I just sacrificed everything for you, so you need to respect me enough to accept this shit. Stop acting fuckin stupid and don't call no damn 911. Let me handle shit my way! You wanted to hit this lick, and I told you I would only be a friend to you, nothing more, nothing less– but if you hit a lick for some money of this magnitude, you have to have a friend you can trust. And I'm the only person on this planet you can trust! Now I need you to trust me in return! Run! Get out of here! Now!"

I had to listen to her even though I didn't want to. I leaned down to kiss her and she spit in my face. "Go!!!!!" She screamed as loud as she could.

I was ripped to shreds inside. My greed had torn my life apart, and destroyed the only thing I ever gave a fuck about. I no longer gave a fuck about the rest of the money. What I had was more than enough because I didn't have shit else to live for. Tears flooded my eyes as I drove down the path to the highway. The entire time I stared at Ms. Lattis, knowing that it was going to be the last time I would ever see her again. Words couldn't describe my level of pain and hurt, and I didn't know what I was going to do with myself or even what destination I was even headed to.

The one thing I'd dreamed of for so long had turned into one of the worst nightmares I could ever live through. I didn't wanna continue living at that point. I considered pulling the gun on myself, but I thought about Ms. Lattis' words again. She sacrificed her life so that I could be free. So that I could live. So I couldn't just take my life, because that wouldn't have been fair to her. At that moment I hated that I told her so much about my plans.

I would have rather died at the hands of my best friend instead of my pride and joy dying at the hands of my best friend. I needed Ms. Lattis more than I needed oxygen. Her prayer, her advice, and her comfort was the only thing that had ever been able to keep me sane through my time on earth. I had no clue what I was going to do without her.

I had nobody left in my corner.

4 YEARS LATER

Today was the most exciting day of my life, as I was finally free from the penitentiary walls. I'd met a guy from my city who called himself MoneyBall Zack, and we got really tight when we realized that our release dates were going to be on the same exact day, in the same exact year. The level of shit I'd learned in prison was priceless. I knew I was going to be a different person once I got out because the government had taught me what it meant to hate.

Before prison, I only understood love, I never even considered hate as an option. I was a working man who wanted to see his people succeed and all have an opportunity to live out the American dream. During my prison bid I learned how America used its' dream as a way to trap African Americans into the nightmare of a harsh reality.

I was locked up with people who were going to be locked up forever. I used to lend my ear and listen to them literally list the list of legitimate things they did for the community compared to to their offense... And I would always shake my head because it made no sense.

My mom was there to pick me up from the bus station once I arrived. She smiled slightly, as though she was happy to see me, but didn't really want to be around me long. Me and her had always had that type of relationship, and that was one of the things that pushed me to start my landscaping business up as soon as I turned 20 years old. I was about to be 27 years old, and many of my childhood friends had passed me by in life. I knew I couldn't get out of prison talking about cutting grass again.

"You been thinking about where you gon work at?" My Mom asked me as soon as I got in her car.
"Wow... I mean... No welcome home? No happy to see me? No how are you doing? Nothing?"

She looked at me and frowned. "Boy this the real world. I been out here working and slaving while you was in there not having a bill to pay. You and the rest of them damn convicts! And you go to jail for some fuckin theft? You know I raised you better than that!"

"Damn so that's what it is huh? You think I'm just like the rest of these niggas right?"

"Well? Ain't cha? What the hell can you do with that stupid ass theft charge on your record? I guess you plan on cutting grass the rest of your damn life! You going down a real stupid path right now. A path I didn't raise you to ever think about, but now you're the got damn spokesperson for the shit."

"Whoa whoa whoa Ma. I'ma need you to respect me and don't talk to me like that."

My mother looked at me with a face full of disgust. "Oh now you gone do something to me? I don't want you in my house boy. Not until you get that convict and felon shit out of your system. And if you never get it out of your system, then you don't never need to stop by my house for no reason whatsoever."

"Damn really? So is that why you never answered my collect calls or wrote me back while I was locked up? That's why you had me worried about you the whole time? Because you felt like I was the scum of the Earth? I couldn't even get a letter Ma?"

My Ma pulled over into a parking lot. "Get out my car nigga. Get out! And get that bag of letters out of my backseat while you're at it. I guess those are letters from your lil criminal Mexican friend since they sent his ass back to Mexico. Y'all had a good opportunity and ruined it beause ya' wanted to *steal*!"

I grabbed the letters and got out of her car. I wasn't in the mood to read no old letters from Jose at that point, I had a lot of shit to figure out in life. The main thing I needed to do was figure out where I was gon' *stay*. I grabbed my plastic bag of items and put the letters from Jose in that bag with the rest of the stuff. I slammed the door and watched as my Mama pressed the gas and mashed out of the parking lot.

I didn't know who to turn do or what I could do, so I went inside the bus station and used their phone to call MoneyBall Zack to see if he could help me any type of way.

"Hello?" An older lady answered.

"Can I speak to Zack?" I asked, not sure if I should have just called him MoneyBall instead.

"Zack! Telephone!" The old lady yelled. "Don't have these people calling my phone all times of the night Zack."

"I'm not going to stay here long Grandma."

"Good! Where ya going then?"

"I'll find somewhere."

"You mean like prison?"

"Oh boy. Hello?" Zack spoke into the phone.

I laughed. "Damn, you going through it just like me I see."

"Oh shit. What's up Patron? Man I was just about to call yo' ass."

"Shit what's up? I'm fucked up. Got no money, nowhere to stay, I'm at ground zero."

"It's gon be good, meet me at the Underground. I got something you gon' like." MoneyBall said.

"Aight, I'm on the way now." I said.

When I got locked up 4 years ago I had a $50 bill in my pocket. When they let me out, I still had that same exact $50 bill. I caught a cab to the Underground and waited on Zack.

***

Zack showed up almost an hour later, somebody in a black Mercedes with tinted windows dropped him off at the red light. After the car drove off I put my hand up in the air so he could see where I was. He walked across the street and handed me a small brown paper bag.

"What's this Zack?" I asked, about to open it up.

"No don't open that shit out here nigga. And don't get caught with it either."

"Well damn nigga what the fuck is this?" I asked him, eager to find out.

"It's a variety pack Patron. It's four 50 slabs in here, and the rest is all dimes and dubs, white and green—"

"Wait, white and green what?"

"Crack and weed nigga!" He yelled in a low voice.

It's a phone in the bag too. If you wanna know how much to sell something for, go to the pictures. I took a picture of the size and I put a price beside every thing in the bag. You'll owe me $800 for this bag."

"$800? What the fuck? I don't got no $800 Zack."

"You gon make about $3,000 nigga. Just post up in this area and you gon get all that shit off. If a police come after you, nigga you better run and don't ever let them recover this phone or the drugs, you hear me?" Zack was speaking without even looking at me.

I really couldn't get mad at him because the man was giving me a chance when my own Mama wouldn't. "Zack how do I let people know I got it?" I was new to the drug game and wanted to make sure I did a good job.

"Man the majority of these people are crackheads brother. They're going to let *you* know you got it. All you gotta do is lean on that wall over there and relax. They're going to walk up to you and look at you crazy. If you don't know what to say, then remember, you can't ever go wrong if you ask them if they're straight or not."

"Are you straight?" I asked.

"No nigga!" Zack answered. "You gotta say.. You Skr8?"

"You skraight?" I repeated.

"Yea that'll work too. But anyways look... You got a couple hours to sell that and I'll bring you some more."

"A couple hours?" *How the hell was I going to do that? That made no sense! I don't have any flyers, no business cards, no types of advertisement material to let people know I'm going to be out here and he wanted me to make $800 worth of sales in a couple of hours?*

The black Benz came back around and came to a stop, waiting on MoneyBall Zack to jump in. "Aight be careful and try to make this shit go fast as possible. I'll see you in a little while." He said and went and jumped in the car.

I walked to the wall that he pointed at and leaned against it. I was opening up the bag when an old man with dirty clothes on and some scars on his face walked up to me.

"Hey." He said and waved at me. He was making me nervous already.

"You skrate?" I asked the old man.

"Shid tryna get skr8 nye! Gottadub?" He asked.

"What color?" I asked.

"Shid ion give a fugg what color it is if it gets me high enough. Shit you know what I want. I wanna dub right nye! I been lookin all ova! Everybody been dry!" He reached in his pocket and pulled out a stack of one dollar bills. "Here you go." He said eagerly.

I looked in the bag and pulled one of the small jewelry bags up with a tiny rock in it. I handed it to him and he frowned. "What the fuck is this? Nigga that ain't no damn dub." He said.

"Oh my fault, I grabbed the wrong." I said as I went back in the bag and got a jewelry bag with a bigger rock in it and handed it to him.

"Oh hell yea! You the best of the best! He took the rock and started running as fast as he could down the sidewalk. I shook my head and pulled the small cell phone out. I pulled the pictures up and instantly shook my head when I realized that I'd just sold the one that went for $50 for $20. This was going to take some getting used to.

I was about to sit down when a group of homeless men and women started walking around the corner talking amongst each other. The same man I'd just sold the rock to walked to the front of the crowd. "They all want a dub man."

"I don't got no more dubs like that. That was a sample." I said, tryna think quick on my feet.
"Shit it don't matter. I'll get what you got." Another man said as he handed me a dirty twenty-dollar bill.

I reached in the bag and found a real dub and handed it to him. He covered it with his fist and walked away quickly. It wasn't long before I'd sold all the dubs for real, and when I didn't have any more dubs, they bought all the dimes. I didn't know how much money I had in total, but I know it was a lot. I'd never made money that fast cutting grass, no matter how tall the weeds had grown.

I had money in all of my pockets, and I needed to get to a quiet, more private area so I could count it. MoneyBall only asked for $800, and I knew I had to have about $4,000 in cash on me. Or maybe it just felt that way. I was doing business so fast that it was scary. I made all that money in one hour! A rush came over me like never before. It was a burst of adrenaline, and it made me think... if I could do that amount in one hour, imagine how much I could make in 24 hours straight nonstop.

I walked to a vacant bench and sat down. I was about to reach and pull my money out when a lady walked up to me pushing a grocery cart full of dirty clothes.

"Excuse me." The older lady said.

I simply looked at her.

"Do you wish to buy a towel? Or a shirt maybe? I have some clean socks for sale in this bag. You don't have to give me much."

Flashbacks of me doing prison time for buying shit off the streets rushed through my brain. I spoke without thinking. "Beat it. Get the fuck away from me. I ain't buying shit!"

The lady put her head down and continued pushing her shopping cart. I reached back in my pocket and pulled my money out. I started trying to straighten it out when out of the corner of my eye I saw the lady approach another guy and trying to sell him a towel. I ignored it and got back to counting my money. Midway through my count, I heard a loud noise.

I looked up and saw the man kick her cart over on the ground and kick it. "I don't want that shit! Get the fuck away from me!" He walked off, and the girl reached over and picked her belongings off of the ground. A part of me felt bad that she was out here bad like that, and despite me getting burned in the past, I had an overwhelming desire to help the old lady.

I walked up to her and helped her get her towels off of the ground. They were dirty, but they still had the tags on them. "You don't have to help me. I'm fine." She said without looking at me.

"You know," I started, "you could really make more money selling towels if they were clean."

She looked at me and frowned. "Well if people would buy them when they were clean, they wouldn't get dirty in my cart!"

I felt bad for her. "How much are your towels?"

"I don't want your money."

She was perplexing. "How old are you?"

"Do it matter? Look go ahead and sell your dope and let me get back to my life."

"And what's your life? What's your name?" I asked her. Something was making me speak to her even when she didn't want to be spoken to.

"I don't have either one. A life or a name."

"Why? What happened to it?"

"It's gone!" She said. "Why are you asking so many questions?"

She looked in my eyes when she asked me that, and an overwhelming feeling of familiarity overcame me. "Because you remind me of this woman I was once in love with. She was like a younger version of you." I said, staring into her eyes.

"Oh yea? What was her name? What happened to her? Why didn't you keep her?" She asked, her hand on her hip.

"I didn't keep her because I never had her. My self-esteem was too low for me to tell her how I felt about her. She had it going on. She was the most beautiful woman I'd ever met in my life... and I was just a man... just another regular... average man who admired her."

"They say looks fade. You probably should have tried at least."

"Looks fade, but I never saw her looks. When I say she was the most beautiful woman I'd ever laid eyes on, I'm saying this to you because it was my first time ever seeing the beauty of another human being's soul. She had the kind of smile that could change a man's life if she smiled at him. She had the kind of voice that would soothe a man's soul if she spoke to him... Much like your voice..."

"Voices are all talk. People use voices and still betray people in the end. People don't mean things they say anymore. Ain't no loyalty."

"But I was loyal to her. If she never met another person who was loyal... I was that person."

"Well I'm sure it would have been better off if you'd have told her instead of keeping it to yourself. Why would you let her go through all that pain if you cared so much about her?"

"Because I was too busy trying to keep her from enduring more pain."

This woman was talking to me like she knew me... As if we knew each other. It was like we were role playing.

"Well you still didn't tell me her name. What does she do?"

"Her name was Ice... She was a booster."

The lady stared at me and a tear fell from her eyes. I couldn't for the life of me understand why the lady was so emotional.

"Why are you crying?" I asked.

"Oh don't mind me. I just enjoy hearing stories like this. When was the last time you saw her?" She asked.

"Oh man... it was years ago... I ended up doing time for her. I used to take my entire check from my job and buy clothes and stuff from her and I never wore the clothes. So I had all of this stolen merchandise in my house. They told me either I testify on her or they were going to charge me with running a theft ring... So I went to prison... It was hard in there, but I made it out... I actually just got out today." I said, almost tearing up.

"Congratulations, and welcome home. What's your name?" She asked me.

"Patrick... but everybody been calling me Patron for years." I said.

"Where's your family Patron? And how do you feel about Ice today, after all you've been through for her?" She studied me carefully.

"I thought about her the whole time I was locked up. I never stopped thinking of her, but I knew I would never see her again. All that time has gone by; she's probably married by now. I had to learn to let go of things I can't control."

"Patron... I'm Ice's biological mother. My name is Sarah. I came up here a few years ago because she'd lost somebody really dear to her. A lady named Ms. Lattis. Before I received the call, Ice was in the streets losing it. She was getting into heavy drug use, just really losing her mind... Me hearing my baby like that made me get my stuff together as best as I could. I came up here and helped her as best as I could. We helped each other... I know you see me out here like this, but trust me, it's more to it than what you see. We deal with a lot of pain to be out here like this. A lot of hurt piled up from so many years. So much betrayal and so many people have crossed us."

I had tears forming in my eyes. "Well I'm not like everybody else Ms. Sarah. I've always loved this woman."

"And I know this woman has always loved you as well. I heard about you when I first got here from Macon, and she always brought you up several times a year. Why don't you follow me so that you can speak to her? We've been all staying in this 1-bedroom place, it's not much of anything, but if you don't mind it... I'll still take you to her."

"I really want nothing more in life but to be able to see her right now."

***

The walk wasn't far at all. We made it to a row of about five 1-bedroom apartments, and I stood there on the outside wiping my tears. I don't know why I was so emotional, but I was. I just couldn't help it... I'd always loved that woman.

A few moments later, the door opened and Ice walked out of the house, just as beautiful as she was the last time I saw her. She stared at me in amazement. I felt myself choking up all over again, not knowing what to say.

"Patron?" She said, with a surprised look on her face.

I nodded my head, unable to speak. Unable to stare at her. It was happening again... I was panicking all over again... I was lost...

"I love you Patron." She said as she walked up to me.

I stared at her in awe. "You love me?" I asked. "Me?"

"Yes... I love you, and only you. I love how you looked out for me when everyone else was trying to take advantage of me... I love how you start to act weird whenever you're around me... I love how protective you are over me... I love how you look at me when you're not even trying to... I love how you were always on time when it was time for you to meet me... There were many things you've done to show me that you really cared for me... So I feel it's only right for me to tell you the truth about how I feel... Sure we have a lot of catching up to do, but if you feel the same way about me today as I feel about you... then we have forever to catch up."

I was stunned, and truly at a lost for words. Ice was misty eyed as she stood before me. Her lips trembling and her hands shaking.

"I love you too Ice... I never in a million years thought I would ever be given the opportunity to tell you those words."

"For some reason, I knew in my heart that I was going to hear those words from you one day... And that's exactly why I saved myself for you and you only."

I wrapped my arms around her and held her as tight as I could. I wanted to protect this woman more than anything, and wanted to be able to give her the world as fast as I could get it.

***

I'd been bonding with Ice all day long. She lay on my chest while she caught me up on everything that had taken place since I last saw her last. I was listening to her and going through Jose's letters at the same time.

"That bitch Reecy Pooh and her nigga Rhondo are living it up off of my money. They got the city locked down, and it's nothing I can do about it." As I listened to her, my mind was spinning. "Baby you already got a cell phone?" She asked.

"Huh?" I had no idea what she was talking about.

She got up and walked to the dresser and picked up the brown bag.

Oh yea that.

"You mind if I answer baby?" She asked me.

"I don't mind at all." I really didn't. I'd forgotten to give him his $800, and had gotten carried away listening to her stories and reading Jose's letters.

"Ah hello? Oh yea well he's busy right now, you can just get it tomorrow. Yea? Well his woman says... he's not leaving her house tonight and you can get it tomorrow ok? Yea."

I was impressed. She came back over and laid up under me again. "That man tripping about some petty $800. I think you should give it all back to him. Every dollar including profit. From experience I know it's better to cut those people off when you still have a chance."

"If I do that, then what will I do? I really wanna' be able to provide for us... I wanna' get us out of this room as soon as possible." It was first on my to-do list.

"Baby I'ma grind with you, I promise you that. All we really need is us... I just need you to love me and never let me down, and I promise the same to you." She said as she kissed my arms.

"I won't let you down Ice. Ever."

We lay there in silence as I continued to read Jose's letters. I sat up when I got halfway through his pile of letters. My eyes bulged out. I couldn't believe what I was reading.

"What baby? What's wrong?" Ice asked, concerned. I decided to read the letter aloud.

"Ok this letter is dated a couple of years ago..." I said, clearing my throat.

Dear Patron,

Hey, this is Jose again. I don't know if your mom will ever give you my letters, but I promise to never stop trying to get in touch with you if it's the last thing I did. Well... like I said in my other letters, my wife bought all this land with the money I was sending her home over the years. Remember you used to tell me that land was gold... So I used to always tell her land was gold... And she went and bought acres upon acres of land out here in Mexico. For the longest I tried my hand in trying to get people to build homes on the land, but I wasn't successful and it was too slow trying to make money from that. So now... I know you got a ways to go before you get home from prison, but just know that I grew my first successful crop of marijuana. I think we just harvested a little over 5,000 pounds on our first try. We fucked up a lot, but we're learning as we go. The same way you gave me a chance when I came to Atlanta is the same way I gave a few men a chance when I got back to Mexico. So they've been believing in me about this marijuana product. I told them that as soon as you got out we would all be rich. They don't believe me.

Jose

"Whoa shit baby!" Ice said as she covered her mouth. "Read one of his latest letters Patron. Let's see the updates."

Dear Patron,

It's been years since we started growing and harvesting marijuana, and at this point, I probably have more marijuana stockpiled than any kingpin. My guys still believe in me, and I told them I think you're about to get out of prison soon, and we would all be rich. They still don't believe me though— well I don't know if they do or don't... they're still around though lol. Anyways, I've been making a living by letting a few people grow on my land, but I told them that as soon as you got out of prison, that will come to a cease. Patron I already have distribution pipelines in place to get you 100,000 pounds of the highest grade marijuana on the market shipped to you whenever you give me the word. According to the research I've done, this amount of weed is worth millions on top of millions, but I'm going to be the same man I was when I came to you on day one, when I first asked you for help. So I'm going to send it to you, and you can tell me what it's worth. You send me however much you think I should get. I don't care one way or the other, the only thing I care about is my loyalty towards you, and I pray that one day you can travel here to see me and my wife and see the empire we've put together waiting on you to come home. I've enclosed my latest phone number. Give me a call as soon as you get this so we can get the ball rolling... You're about to be the most powerful man in America, I promise you that.

Jose

PATRON

I used some of the money I'd made earlier and paid for two hotel rooms at the Westin Peachtree Plaza. I got one room for Mom, and one room for me and my future wife. There was no doubt about it... I was going to marry that woman. We both knew that it was inevitable. I asked her why her Mom was out trying to sell towels earlier, and she told me that her Mom had to have something to do in order to keep her sanity. To her it wasn't about the actual product, it was just about having a positive activity. I made a mental note to invest in her a business as soon as I could. I couldn't let her keep doing that.

Ice stood in the floor to ceiling window and admired the beautiful view of one of America's most powerful cities. "It's such a beautiful view Patron."

"But not more beautiful than the view I have." I said as I walked up behind her and wrapped my arms around her. "I love you baby." I whispered in her ear gently.

"I love you too Patron."

She turned around and kissed me, our connection as powerful as an electrical outlet, her touch more wonderful than life itself— her eyes a reflection of the glow of her heart, her smile an autograph worth a million pounds of gold. I loved this woman, and I was going to make sure that she understood that for as long as I lived. I was thankful for this woman, amazed that a black man with as many flaws as myself could be afforded the opportunity to stand in the presence of one of the most perfectly constructed pieces of chocolate this world had ever seen.

I'd sacrificed my life for this woman once in the past, and the only reason I'd be hesitant to do it again, was because I'd risk not being with her for a moment. I never wanted that to happen. I wanted to give her my heart in a protective case and with a warranty, a promise, and a guarantee attached to it. I wanted her to have my last name, and I wanted it to mean something to her. I wanted several forevers, but I would only accept the forevers if it included her for every second.

She pressed against my body and reached down for my belt, and I stopped her. I moved her hand out the way and kissed her gently.

"Ice... You said you've been saving yourself right?" I asked softly.

"For you... this whole time." She replied, breathing frantically.

"Then we should get married tomorrow and make it right. I wanna' show you that I'm for real about you. If tomorrow's too soon, then I understand, and I'm willing to wait until you're ready." I said nervously.

"Tomorrow can't come quick enough." Ice's face was flush with happiness. She bit her bottom lip and shook her head. "Oh yea... tomorrow really can't come quick enough Patron. And I've been thinking about that letter you read me... The one from your friend Jose."

"Yea? What about it?" I asked curiously.

"I'll only feel comfortable if we do it as a couple. You might not know it now, but you'll know it soon... I'm gon' forever be the realest one on your team."

I smiled at her. "Baby I wouldn't have it any other way. I already know we're perfect for each other. You got my back and I damn sure got yours. I won't ever let anybody cross you, and I know you feel the same about me. Real black love, no games. Forget a Bonnie and Clyde, we're about to be the first couple of the trap."

Author's Notes

I've said thank you a million times, and I'll continue to say it each and every time you support me. I'll be the first to tell you that I've dropped the ball over the years trying to balance my companies and trying to have a career as an author at the same time. Some people may see it as though I didn't work hard enough... But if you would have been in my shoes, you'd have probably shut down and had breakdowns the same way I did. However, I'm honestly in a great mental space right now. I haven't been at this level of happiness in years, therefore I'm able to create freely again. I'm still very passionate about writing, still excited about literature, the only thing I'll ask... please leave me a review on Amazon. That's literally the only motivating factor I have sometimes— the feedback from readers. In the past, if I put out a book and it didn't get as much feedback, then I assumed that readers don't want to hear more in that series. Let's make a deal... leave reviews, and I'll work as hard as I need to in order to give you whatever it is you're asking for. Thank you for supporting me, I'm forever grateful. Text TBRS to 95577 for updates.

Made in the USA
San Bernardino, CA
19 August 2017